Homicide on the

Homestead

Nanci M. Pattenden

Homicide on the Homestead

Copyright © 2021 Nanci M. Pattenden

This is a work of fiction. All characters, names, incidents, organizations, and dialogue in this novel are either the products of the author's imagination or are used fictitiously.

Published by Murder Does Pay, Ink
Ontario, Canada
www.murderdoespayink.ca

ISBN: 978-1-7770778-1-5

1 2 3 4 5 6 7 8 9 0

Detective Hodgins Victorian Murder Mysteries

Body in the Harbour

Death on Duchess Street

Corpses for Christmas

Books 1 to 3 Collection

Homicide on the Homestead

D.E.M.ON. Tales Series

Assassin Eco-Corpses

Bobcat Got Your Tongue?

A Craptacular Understatement

ACKNOWLEDGMENTS

I'd like to say a great big thanks to Omar and Ashley, owners of Cardinal Press Espresso Bar in Newmarket for providing a wonderful environment in which to work. They have a lovely big room in the back of their coffee shop, creating the perfect place to call "my office."

As always, thanks to my editor, MJ, of Infinite Pathways, and Chris, my graphics guru.

THANK YOU

CHAPTER ONE

Detective Hodgins couldn't wait for Constable Barnes' sweetheart to return from her trip to Europe. The poor lad's jaw almost hit the floor when Violet's father made the announcement at the Christmas Eve party. Instead of proposing after Christmas, as Barnes planned, he kept his gob shut. Only Hodgins and his wife knew what the young man had planned. For the past five months Barnes had moped about, anxious, depressed, and generally a pain in the arse. All in all, it was a pretty grim start to 1875.

Barnes stood at Hodgins' office door, pulled a wrinkled letter from his trouser pocket, and waved it in the air. "This came in the last post yesterday. Violet mailed it before getting on the steam ship home. Thought she'd never return."

Hodgins leaned back in his chair, glad the young constable's moaning would finally end. "You must be over the moon. Now you'll be able to propose." Hodgins' smile faded as he noticed the look on Barnes' face. "Why aren't you happy?"

"It's the letter, sir. I think she may already be betrothed. Maybe even wed. In her last several letters she went on ever so much about a nobleman her aunt had introduced her to." Barnes crumpled into the chair in front of the desk, his hand clenching the letter, adding several more wrinkles.

"Did she say this nobleman was courting her?"

Barnes shrugged. "Not in so many words, but she seemed fascinated with him. A nobleman! How can a dull constable compete with that?"

"Don't be so hard on yourself, Henry."

Their conversation ended abruptly when a local businessman rushed into Station House Four.

"Help, come quick. He's got a gun. Please, hurry."

Hodgins tried to calm him and get more information. "Who has a gun? Take a deep breath and start from the beginning. Is anyone injured?"

The man took a few deep breaths. "Some fool's waving a revolver around down by Prescott Brewing. Ain't shot no one yet, far as I know."

Hodgins pointed at two constables as they prepared to hit their beats. "You two, go find that fool, and bring him in for disturbing the peace. Anything to get him off the street. And make damn sure one of you gets that gun."

Barnes started to leave, but Hodgins waved him back.

The lad was too distracted to be dealing with some idiot waving a gun. Probably end up getting himself and a few others shot. "Not you, Henry. I need you here to go over the notes on the floater pulled from the Don River yesterday. Still don't know who she is."

"Yes, sir. She was dressed like a scullery maid, so I've put word out among a few servants from the large homes along the river. No one's reported anyone missing yet. I'll follow up on a few of them. See if anyone's heard anything new."

Hopefully talking to some pretty young maids would take his mind off Violet. If that girl came back married or engaged, he didn't want to think how Barnes would react.

* * *

An hour passed before the constables returned, a foul odour following them.

"Where's the man who caused the ruckus?" The downcast eyes lead Hodgins to his own conclusion. "Got away, didn't he? And what is that god-awful smell?"

"He ran off when he saw us. Constable Green talked to the witnesses and I went after him. Chased him through an alley by the brewery and ran smack dab into a rubbish pile. Last I saw, he hopped on the streetcar. Got a description, though."

Crawford opened his notebook and took a few steps

away from Green and the less than pleasant aroma. "Early twenties, dark hair, wearing dungarees, and rubber boots. One man got close enough to see mole by the right ear. No one admitted to knowing him. The man waved the gun around, fired a few shots in the air, then bolted when we arrived."

He paused and took a few more steps away. "One woman fainted. Don't appear no one got hurt."

Hodgins cringed at the grammar. Too many uneducated men on the force. He hoped that changed in the future. "Well, as long as nobody's injured, there's not much we can do, unless someone files a complaint. The lady who fainted, she's all right? Didn't hurt herself when she fell?"

"Fainted into her husband's arms. Came around right quick and they continued on their way. He had a few choice words, though."

"Complimenting the Toronto Constabulary, I have no doubt. Write it up and go about your rounds." He pointed at Green. "You. Change first."

* * *

Hodgins arrived home earlier than usual as the day was, for the most part, uneventful. He also wanted to get away from Barnes' long face and constant sighs. Finding the identity of the drowned girl was the only positive thing all day.

The sounds of a happy family greeted Hodgins when he

opened the front door. A barking dog and crying babies, while not the most pleasant sounds one would want to hear after a long day at work, reminded Hodgins of all he had. A beautiful wife, loving daughter, faithful dog, and now twin girls, almost two, the most recent additions to the family.

Up until a month ago, his home had been even more lively. Fortunately, his brother, Jonathan, finally moved into a house of his own, taking his wife and two children with them. They still practically lived with Hodgins, though. Jonathan had found a house on Cumberland, a few blocks away. Shortly after the new year, he'd opened his export business on Front Street, not far from the harbour and Union Station. Hodgins admired his brother's determination to turn his life around.

Hodgins followed the sounds of the toddlers into the front room, smiling as he watched his eldest, Sara, with the twins. She sat beside her old home-made playpen, getting ready to feed them. So grown up for a ten year old. Sara acted more like their mother than a sister, insisting on the Christmas names she'd picked. Holly and Ivy. He only hoped neither of the twins grew up to be anything like their natural born parents.

Hodgins had left instructions with the prison to be notified when their mother gave birth and to be told when the baby was adopted, but he held little hope they'd bother to inform him. Since Sara didn't require his help, he continued to the kitchen, wondering why the dog hadn't run to the door when he arrived. The aroma of roast chicken filled the room.

"You're early. Supper won't be ready for at least thirty minutes, Bertie. Why don't you take Scraps for a walk? He's been underfoot all afternoon. I had to put him in the yard." Scraps barked and ran to the back porch when he spotted Hodgins through the window.

Hodgins wrapped his arms around his wife's waist and kissed Delia's cheek. "Trying to get me out of the way as well?"

"Never, but he could use a good long walk. Wear him out. I don't want him keeping the twins awake again."

* * *

Next morning Hodgins arrived at an unusually quiet station. Unfortunately, it didn't last long. He'd almost managed to finish his tea when the front door slammed against the wall as a man wearing overalls and muddy rubber boots rushed in.

"He's dead – Murdered. Someone help!"

Hodgins came out and led the man into his office, motioning for Barnes to bring in some tea. "Calm down, sir. Who's dead? Tell me what happened. Are you certain it wasn't an accident?"

"Aren't you listening? Weren't no accident. Bucky was murdered."

"Bucky?" Hodgins took a pad of long paper from his desk drawer. "Can you give me his full name please?"

The farmer pulled a checkered hanky from his overalls and wiped his face. "Elmer Buckingham. Everyone calls him Bucky."

Barnes rapped on the door frame and entered. He set a cup of tea in front of the man, then looked at Hodgins. "Top up, sir?"

Hodgins shook his head and waved Barnes away.

"Take a deep breath, have some tea, then tell me exactly what happened. Start with your name."

Slightly more relaxed after a few sips, the man set the cup back on the desk. "Daniel Logan. I'm neighbour to Bucky. Went over this morning to see if there was anything he needed help with. He's quite old. Took the wife with me so she could have a natter with Lenore, Mrs. Buckingham. Went out to the barn to chat with Bucky and found him just inside the door." He stopped and had a bit more tea. "Worst thing I ever did see. Blood splattered all over. Shut the door, told the wife to keep Eleanor away from the barn and drove the team hard into town."

Hodgins wrote as Logan relayed the information, not looking up until the farmer stopped talking. "Where exactly are your farms?"

"Other side of the tracks, a bit north of Kingston Road, off Robinson. If you see the cemetery, you've gone too far. Please hurry."

"I'll send for the coroner, and ride out with you myself." Hodgins tore a sheet off the pad. "Here, draw out a map so the coroner doesn't get lost. He's new and doesn't know his way around the city, never mind the outlying areas."

Hodgins took the sketch and went over to Barnes' desk. "Fetch Dr. Stonehouse. Sounds like another murder. It's a bit out of the city, so you'll probably need this. Come out with the doctor. Oh, tell him to bring some laudanum. Victim's wife could probably use it." He gave Barnes the map and headed out with Logan.

By the time they reached the farm, Hodgins knew more than he cared to about Elmer and Lenore Buckingham. If what Logan said was true, it seemed impossible anyone would want to harm either of them. As they approached the house, sobbing broke the silence of the countryside.

"Dagnabbit. Tol' my wife to keep Lenore away from the barn." He pointed to the large structure several feet away, door wide open. "I closed that before I left. Not fit for a woman to see, 'specially it being her husband and all."

He stopped the horses in front of the porch and tied the reins to a rail. "Ain't never gonna get her calmed down now."

"Dr. Stonehouse should be bringing something for her nerves. I'm sure your wife can take care of her until he arrives. I need to see the victim." Hodgins followed Logan's gaze to the open barn door. "You stay here while I check the barn. Don't want anything disturbed."

Logan let out a shallow breath of relief. His colour had faded noticeably. The corner of Hodgins' mouth twitched as he thought about Barnes' similar reaction to murder victims. When the detective arrived at the barn, he understood. All doubt about this being a simple accident vanished. It was pure carnage. Stonehouse would have his work cut out for him trying to determine cause of death. Hodgins readied himself then knelt beside the body.

"Beginning to feel a bit like Barnes," he told the horse in the nearby stall.

Hodgins examined the body best he could, not wanting to disturb anything until the coroner arrived. What appeared to be a bullet hole surrounded by a massive red stain sat directly over the man's heart. Hodgins pulled at the corner of his moustache as he thought. A wound like that certainly killed the poor bugger instantly. Why did someone bother to take the time to bash Buckingham's face in?

The elderly man lay flat on his back, arms at his sides. No defensive wounds were evident on his hands. Whoever it was, Buckingham knew and probably trusted the man. There was no way a woman could have done that much damage, even with the man flat on his back. The splatter would have gone everywhere. Someone must be walking around covered in blood. The blood! As he stood, a warm feeling seeped through his trousers and onto his legs.

"Blast!" Both pant legs were saturated from the knees down. He'd been concentrating so much on the body he wasn't aware of his surroundings. Now, that's all he noticed.

A rag hung on a nail by the stalls. By the time he finished wiping off his trousers, the rag had turned from dingy white to a darkish pink. Unfortunately, the stickiness didn't come out.

"Hello? Sir, are you out here?"

Hodgins turned just as Barnes and Dr. Stonehouse entered the barn. Barnes took one quick look at the body and ran out.

"Where's he off to in such a hurry?" The doctor watched as Barnes disappeared from sight.

Hodgins grinned. "He'll be back in a minute. As you can see, the victim is right there. I'm guessing from the amount of blood and the hole over his heart, he died from the shot."

"You're probably right, but do you mind if I have a look for myself?"

"That's what you're here for. Mind the blood. Got the blasted stuff all over me. Maybe we could lay some of that straw around the body? No point both of us going home a bloody mess."

"Good idea." Together they pulled handfuls of straw from one of the bales and placed it beside the body.

Barnes returned, a little paler than usual.

Hodgins grinned. "Why don't you go inside and take some statements? Find out if anyone heard anything. Ask when the last time was anyone saw him."

"Yes, sir. Thank you."

"The wife should be calmer." The doctor placed his black bag on a nearby bale of hay. "Stopped at the house first and left a bottle of laudanum.

Stonehouse knelt beside the body and unbuttoned the shirt. Hodgins hovered over his shoulder. The doctor took a cloth from his bag and gently wiped the blood from the man's chest.

"What the hell is that?" Hodgins asked. Instead of a bullet wound, as expected, there were four holes.

CHAPTER TWO

"That's the work of a very disturbed person, I'd say." Stonehouse pointed at one hole that was different. "As you said, bullet probably killed him. Would have bled out fast. These other holes? I grew up on a farm, and I'd hazard a guess they were made by a pitchfork. Didn't you notice the extra holes in the shirt?"

"I was concentrating more on the damage to his face." Hodgins looked around. "Don't see a pitchfork anywhere. Might be hidden, or possibly the murderer took it with him."

"I'll need to bring the body to the morgue and examine him properly."

"Yes, of course. I'll grab a blanket or something from the house to cover him and help you get him in the wagon. Then Barnes can go through the barn with me if he's sufficiently recovered."

The doctor raised an eyebrow. "Recovered?"

"Weak stomach." As Hodgins made his way to the house, he heard Stonehouse mumble something.

Hodgins returned with a white sheet, Barnes and Logan close behind. With Barnes' assistance, Hodgins maneuvered Mr. Buckingham into the back of the doctor's wagon.

Dr. Stonehouse climbed onto the buckboard. "I'll have a preliminary report for you by the end of the day." He snapped the reins, and the grey Newfoundland pony trotted forward.

After they watched the doctor turn the wagon around, Hodgins addressed Barnes. "How's Mrs. Buckingham doing?"

Logan answered before Barnes could open his mouth. "My Rose gave her a dose of the doctor's medicine and sent her to bed. She'll be out for a fair bit, I'd say. The dose was rather large."

Hodgins nodded to Barnes. "I need you to help me go through the barn."

"Right away, sir."

"And, Mr. Logan, if you wouldn't mind, when we're through here, could you take us back to town? I'm afraid we've been left stranded."

"Lost most of the day already. Few more hours ain't gonna make much difference now." Logan let the screen door slam shut behind him.

"We can search the barn now that the body's been moved." Hodgins started walking, but Barnes didn't follow.

"Come on , lad. Take a deep breath and tell me what you found out. It'll take your mind off what you saw."

"Yes, sir. Barnes caught up to the detective and they continued to the barn.

"Didn't find out much that can help. They've a hired hand, but he's been out in the fields all day. Not much of a working farm any longer. The children have grown and moved away. A son and a daughter. The son lives on the next concession. The daughter is in the city, at least she was. Mrs. Buckingham mentioned they were planning to move. She's too distraught to recall where or when. I suppose we'll need to contact them."

"Yes, I think that's best. From the sounds of it, she's probably not up to telling them herself. If the son's not far, maybe Mr. Logan can fetch him. You start looking around, and I'll talk to Logan. Leave it up to him what to tell the son. Maybe the son's wife can tell her sister-in-law, or at least be there when she's told."

Hodgins walked back to the porch and called for Logan. "Since you know the son and where his farm is, would you mind fetching him? Mrs. Buckingham needs her family around her."

Logan muttered something Hodgins couldn't make out, but he nodded and went to the barn.

Hodgins stood beside Barnes after Logan took the

Buckingham's horse, watching him gallop across the fields to fetch the dead man's son.

"He's rather grumpy, but at least he's helpful," Barnes said.

"That he is. Maybe a bale of hay from the livery will put him in a better mood. For all his help."

"What exactly are we looking for?"

"Buckingham was shot, punctured with a pitchfork, and bashed about the head with something. We're looking for any or all of those items. Whoever did this most likely took the gun with him, but the pitchfork should be around somewhere, as well as whatever was used on his head."

Barnes put a hand to his mouth.

"Again?"

Barnes swallowed. "No, sir."

"Don't feel bad. Almost puked myself. Now, you look around the loft and I'll go through the stalls."

Hodgins started with the empty ones. The Buckingham's only had two horses, and Mr. Logan rode one of them. The other stalls were either swept clean, or used to store bales and buckets. One had a pair of old overalls hanging on a nail, a pair of muddy rubber boots sitting below. Nothing was hidden behind any of the bales and they all seemed undisturbed. A quick check into the buckets revealed nothing more than an old bird nest.

The now empty horse stall was covered with a fresh layer of straw, slightly soiled by the mare. A small trough partially filled with hay sat in the corner, and a bucket of water hung on a nail a few feet away. Hodgins kicked the straw around, looking for anything hidden beneath. Nothing. He saved the stall with the draft horse for last. Hodgins walked around carefully, not wanting to startle the large horse, even though it looked old, and seemed quite gentle. The contents were much the same, with nothing hidden inside.

"Find anything yet, Barnes?"

"Just a litter of kittens in the far corner and a few mice."

After another hour of checking, neither found anything that could have been used to kill Buckingham. They'd just begun exploring the area outside the barn when Logan returned.

"Charlie's coming along the road with his wife. Should be here soon. Told him there'd been trouble. Left the details for you to fill in." Logan took the horse back into the barn and settled her into her stall before going inside.

"You'd think he'd be more curious, what with them being neighbours and all," Barnes said.

"I noticed that, too. Maybe he's just not the nosey sort. I'm glad he's not underfoot, but maybe we'd best check into his background. Keep looking around. Can't image someone walked off carrying a bloody pitchfork. It's got to be here somewhere."

Barnes barely rounded the corner of the barn when he let out a holler. "Over here. I found it."

A well-used pitchfork lay in the dirt a few feet beyond the barn. The paint on the handle had faded but the tines glistened with fresh blood.

Hodgins picked it up and walked over to the front porch, propping it against the rail.

"Wish we had our own wagon so we didn't have to leave this out in plain sight. Don't want Mrs. Buckingham to come out and see it, or the son for that matter. This happened recently. Blood's barely begun to dry. Not a pleasant sight."

Barnes pointed down the lane. "Looks like the son's coming now."

A cloud of dust kicked up behind the buggy; the woman in the front hanging on for dear life. The horse reared as it was pulled to a stop beside Hodgins and Barnes. Hodgins reached up, grabbed the bridle, then stroked the horse's nose to settle it down. A man in his fifties leapt down.

"Who are you? What's this trouble Daniel spoke of?"

Barnes rushed around the buggy and helped the women down. The pins had come loose and several dust-filled strands of hair stuck out at odd angles. "Is Mother

Buckingham all right? Mr. Logan wouldn't say a word."

Hodgins showed his badge to Charlie. I'm Detective Hodgins, Toronto Constabulary. This is Constable Barnes. I'm very sorry to inform you that your father has been killed."

Without uttering a sound, the young Mrs. Buckingham fainted. Her husband grabbed her before she hit the ground.

Barnes held the door as she was carried inside. Her husband placed her on the settee, then dropped onto on ottoman. "Father? Dead? How?"

"Can we talk in the kitchen? Mrs. Logan, can you tend to the young lady?"

Mrs. Logan pushed some stray grey hairs off her face and tucked them into the bun at the back of her head. She sat on the ottoman vacated by Charlie.

Once the men were separated from the woman, Hodgins asked Barnes to make some tea for everyone. For some reason, people seemed to settle down a bit with the distraction of a hot drink.

"This won't be pleasant to hear. Did your father have any enemies? A disagreement with someone perhaps?" Hodgins asked.

"No, no one. My father was one of the most gentle people you'd meet. Everyone liked him. Why would you think he had an enemy?"

"As I said, this isn't pleasant. Not only was he shot, but someone stabbed him with a pitchfork, and beat him about the head. We haven't determined what with yet."

Charlie Buckingham blanched. "My God. Why would anyone do such a thing?" He sat up straight. "Mother! Where is she? Has she been injured?"

"No, she's fine, just shaken up. The doctor left laudanum for her. She's sleeping."

Charlie slumped in the chair. "Thank God."

"Barnes, do you know when Mr. Buckingham was last seen?"

Barnes flipped through the pages of his notebook. "Yes, his wife saw him mid-morning. He'd been cleaning the barn and she took him a slice of fresh bread."

"What about the hired hand?" Hodgins asked. "What's his name?"

"Smitty," Charlie said. "Gabriel Smith. He's almost as old as Father."

Hodgins nodded to Barnes, indicating for him to take notes. "How long has he worked here?"

Charlie shrugged. "Not sure. Five, maybe six years."

"And he got on with your folks?"

"He was on friendly enough terms with them. Kept to himself. Don't really know much about him. I never had any reason to think he was trouble, though." Charlie snorted

19

and shook his head. "He's just a stupid old man my father took pity on. Two old fools trying to run a farm. Run it into the ground, more like."

Hodgins stood. "I don't think there's anything else at the moment. I would like to speak with your mother when she's recovered from the shock. Meanwhile, if you find or see anything suspicious, send for an officer right away. And don't touch anything that might have been used to harm him. We found the pitchfork and will be taking that with us." He turned to Logan. "If you wouldn't mind taking us back to the station?"

A slight moan and the sounds of a woman stirring came from the sitting room. "I believe your wife has recovered." Hodgins bowed slightly to Charlie. "We'll leave you to grieve."

CHAPTER THREE

Few words were spoken on the ride back to Toronto, but Mr. Logan's mood improved a little when Hodgins gave him a chit for a bale of fresh hay from John Mitchel's livery. When they entered the station, Hodgins poured a cup of tea and motioned for Barnes to follow him into his office. Barnes sat in the chair opposite the desk, waiting for Hodgins to settle in and retrieve his pad of paper from the desk drawer.

"One thing seems peculiar about this murder." Hodgins tapped his pencil on the pad of foolscap.

"Nothing missing. Not one person said anything had been stolen." Barnes slid to the edge of the chair and leaned on the desk. "Why kill someone and not take anything?"

"Exactly. Whoever did this didn't even take the gold band from Buckingham's finger. That would be easily pawned, maybe even melted. Blacksmith's shop would have a hot enough fire."

Barnes sat back. "I don't believe anyone lied to us. They all seemed quite sincere. Didn't like the son, though. Don't take much stock in men who are so thoughtless towards women, especially their wife. Did you see the state of her after that buggy ride? And he didn't even help her down."

Hodgins laughed. "Wait 'til you've been married a few years. We men tend to forget that woman expect us to act as though we're still courting. And rightly so. Unfortunately, many women don't realize that it goes both ways. I know I certainly don't like to be ignored and taken for granted."

Barnes slumped in the chair. "Wouldn't know anything about that," he mumbled.

Hodgins silently berated himself. "Sorry, lad. When did you say she was returning?"

"Thursday. Three very long days away."

"Don't know why you've gotten yourself into such a tizzy. Did she even once say she was infatuated with this Duke?"

"Nobleman, sir. And no. But she did go on about him."

"Describe him in detail at all?"

Barnes shook his head.

"Well, there you go. Probably a doddering old man with a lifetime of interesting stories. My wife has been talking with Violet's mother. Hearing all about the trip from the letters she's received from her sister-in-law. Nary a word about anything romantic going on with Violet. Got all sorts of ideas in Cordelia's head about us taking a trip to Europe.

Too bad she doesn't have any siblings. Could send them off on their own. Not that a trip to Paris or Rome wouldn't be nice. Just can't take the time off. Maybe when the twins are older."

Hodgins picked up his pencil, holding it over the pad of paper. "Now, tell me what other information you got while I was with the coroner."

Barnes had his notebook ready; half of the pages still crisp and clean.

"Let's see. The Buckingham's rose when the sun came up, just like every day, apparently. The hired hand, Gabriel Smith, arrived shortly after and they all had breakfast. Smith went out to work in the fields, and Buckingham went to the barn. Mrs. Buckingham did the dishes, went out to the vegetable garden to water the seedlings, then back inside to do her daily chores. Headed to the barn mid-morning with a slice of fresh bread for her husband, then went back inside to do some mending. That's about all until the neighbour came calling and found Buckingham dead in the barn."

Hodgins wrote as Barnes spoke, continuing with his own notes long after the constable stopped talking. Finally, Hodgins put his pencil down and looked at Barnes.

"So many questions. We need to find out more about this Smith fellow. How does he know the Buckinghams? Where did he work before? Why did he leave? And the son.

What was his relationship with his father really like? Wouldn't be the first time a child killed for an inheritance. Looks like the Buckinghams have a fair-sized property." He paused for a sip of tea, then started sketching the farm. "The laneway comes up to the house." He drew a box. "And the barn's just east." Another box. Hodgins drew two arrows. "Son's over that way, and the fields are north. No other roads out, but plenty of trees around."

"Shall I find out about that neighbour?"

"Yes. See if he's in the habit of just popping in for a visit. Could there be a squabble no one has bothered to tell us about? And I suppose we should look into the daughter. Her husband might not be the nicest, and want the property. They live in the city so they won't have much land. Did you find out if they've moved?"

"Just moved last week. Over Kleinberg way. Shall I go back out now and ask more questions, sir?"

"No, leave the family be. It can wait until tomorrow. I'll need another constable or two so we can cover more ground. I'll prepare a list of names and questions and send you and Harrington out in the morning. Check and see who else is working tomorrow. I'll speak with the son-in-law myself. I doubt he'll know much more."

Barnes stood and headed to the door. "I'll see if I can find anything on the son and son-in-law. Maybe they've been on the wrong side of the law at some point. Smith too."

Hodgins made more notes, doodled while he thought, and wrote while mumbling. "The three constables can take a buggy from the livery and go out to the farm. Harrington can talk to Logan, Barnes is familiar with the Buckingham property, so he can talk to them again. The other constable can go out to the son's farm. Maybe Riddell. Reliable, and he always takes good notes. Hope he's on tomorrow's schedule." He looked up and called to Barnes, waving him to return to the office.

Hodgins pulled the much-used train schedule from the back of his desk drawer and flattened it out. Running his finger down the list of stops, he swore when he couldn't find Kleinberg. He thought for a moment then snapped his fingers. *Toronto, Grey & Bruce Line.* He opened his drawer and rooted around, finally pulling out a near pristine schedule.

"Ah, here it is. Naturally, the train is an early one. Why the devil can't they run the trains more often?"

"Sir?" Barnes stood in the doorway, listening as Hodgins talked to himself.

Hodgins glanced up. "Just a minute." He tore a clean sheet from the pad and organized his list, then handed it to Barnes on the way out. "I'll be going straight to Union

Station in the morning. Here's what I need you, Harrington, and hopefully Riddell, to do tomorrow. Should be back by four. If you're here when I return, we can review everything. If not, I'll meet with all three of you the next day."

Hodgins put his notes in the desk drawer and headed home, wanting to get an early night for change. He walked, using the time to mull over the information they had.

When he arrived, he went into the kitchen to watch while Cordelia prepared their supper. Sara and her cousins played in the backyard with the dog. The children had been coming over after school most days to allow his sister-in-law, Elizabeth, more time to get their new house in order.

"I hope you don't mind, but I've told Elizabeth the children can spend the night. She and Jonathan have had so little time together since they moved back. I thought a quiet night would do them good."

"Of course I don't mind. You know as well as I do they have more than a few issues they need to work out. Might not be a bad idea to have Cora and Freddie spend the weekend."

He filled the kettle and placed it on the wood-burning stove before taking two tea cups from the cupboard. Cordelia stopped chopping carrots and turned to him.

"Two cups? Is there something you need to discuss, Bertie?"

"Yes. There's been a murder on the other side of The Don. Elderly man. Rather brutal."

Cordelia continued preparing the vegetables until the kettle boiled, then joined her husband at the table to hear the story.

"Oh, that's horrible. Why would anyone kill a harmless old man? How disgusting."

Hodgins blew on his steaming tea before taking a sip. "Yes, it is rather disgusting. Won't tell you the details, but on the surface, it seems as though he was well liked. I'll be heading to Kleinberg in the morning to speak with his daughter and son-in-law. Can't image they'd have found out yet, unless a telegram was sent. Rather impersonal, though. I suppose it's possible her brother could have taken a team up, but he didn't strike me as the sort who'd go out of his way. Might have taken the evening train, but he'd have to stay over. I'll find out when I get there. Never did like having to tell people someone close to them died, never mind murdered."

The children charged through the door, led by the dog, cutting the conversation short. Everyone was caked in mud. The ground still hadn't dried from the heavy rain the day before. Hodgins herded them back into the porch so Cordelia could finish preparing the evening meal.

"Off with your shoes, the lot of you. And don't move

until I find some towels and clean clothes." He rounded up the dog and put him with the children before going upstairs to find them something to wear. Hodgins returned to find his wife cleaning the muddy paw prints off the floor.

"Leave that to me, you just take care of the food." He opened the porch door wide enough to pass the clothing and towels through, then relieved Delia of the mop and bucket. "I'd rather clean a mess then eat late." He winked at his wife and finished the floor, then retired to the sitting room to read the newspaper before supper.

* * *

Hodgins rose early the next morning, leaving enough time to stop at his brother's home to say they'd keep Cora and Freddie all weekend. He was surprised to find his sister-in-law already up, as he intended to simply slip a note under their door.

"Good Morning, Elizabeth. You're up early." He handed her the note. "Just wanted to let you know we'll keep the children over the weekend. Give you more time to, um, sort things out.

She took the note. "Thank you, Albert. Jonathan promised to stay out of trouble. Come in. He'll be down shortly."

"Sorry, but I've got a train to catch. We'll have you all over to dinner one evening soon." He tipped his hat then rushed out and down to Bloor Street, hailing a hansom at the corner.

"Union Station. Quick as you can."

The horses galloped at a good speed, as not many people were up and about yet. He made the train with five minutes to spare; just enough time to pick up the early edition of *The Globe*. One delay and he'd be wasting a full day before speaking to the daughter. A newsboy stood outside Union Station, so he bought the paper before going inside to purchase his ticket.

With an hour and a half ride to Kleinberg, he had plenty of time to peruse the news. He cringed when reading about the man who jumped from an engine on the Grand Trunk and ended up losing his foot. As he read about Detective Burrow's robbery, Hodgins yawned, wishing it was Burrows who had to come in early instead of him. At least the day promised to be pleasant. He always enjoyed May, watching everything spring to life. The rhyme April showers bring May flowers popped to mind. They certainly had more than enough rain in April to bring plenty of flowers this month.

The write-up about the fire by Queen's Wharf caught his attention. At least it wasn't close to his brother's business. Too many fires by the waterfront lately. One carelessly flung fag or cigar caused far too much damage, and took more lives than he cared to recall. A few had been started on purpose. He folded the paper, tucked it in his coat pocket, leaned back, and dozed.

The shrill whistle woke him as the train pulled into Kleinberg.

He wasn't surprised to find the station a fair ways out of town and, naturally, had a tavern nearby. He asked the station master if he knew where the McTaggart's lived, hoping new residents would've been a topic of conversation around town. A farmer loading supplies off the train overheard and offered him a ride into town.

"Heard about the new folks. Bought a place not far from the Methodist Church. Opening up a chemist shop. We'll have two. Imagine! Town's really starting to grow. Ever bin up here afore?"

Hodgins shook his head. "No, don't really have much time to travel about. It's nice when I have the opportunity to visit small towns like this, unfortunately it's usually business, and not very pleasant."

Most of the thirty-minute ride into town was so bumpy Hodgins accidently bit his tongue – more than once. The farmer just chatted on about the town, and how it was growing, completely oblivious to the rough ride. Regrettably, he couldn't provide any information on the McTaggart's as no one in town knew them yet. The farmer pulled the rig to a halt shortly after they passed the church, and pointed.

"That little house there is where the new folks live."

Hodgins thanked him for the ride, walked up the steps, and knocked. A woman about forty-five opened the door, her hair hidden under a bandana, a dirty apron tied around her waist. She seemed in fine spirits, humming softly and smiling. Hodgins assumed the news had not reached Kleinberg.

"Mrs. McTaggart?"

"Yes, please come in. What can I do for you?"

Hodgins stepped inside and closed the door behind him. "Is your husband at home?"

"No, he's readying his new shop. As you can see, we've recently moved." She motioned to the unopened crates in the front room. "He's opening a chemist's shop. I can give you directions."

Hodgins hesitated, not certain what to do. He didn't wish to tell her that her father had been murdered if no one was home to sit with her. He pulled back the lapel of his jacket, revealing his badge.

"I'm Detective Hodgins, Toronto Constabulary. I have some rather disturbing news. It might be best if I fetch your husband. I had rather hoped your brother might have come up already."

"My brother? You're scaring me, Detective. Please tell

me what's wrong."

"Don't mean to frighten you, but I think I'd rather wait until your husband is here. Where might I find him?"

Mrs. McTaggart directed him toward a shop just around the corner. She stood in the doorway watching Hodgins as he hurried to the chemist's. She still stood in the doorway when they returned.

"Joseph, you look a fright. Whatever is wrong?"

Her husband lead her into the front parlour to one of the chairs that wasn't blocked by crates.

"It's your father. I'm afraid he's dead."

CHAPTER FOUR

Hodgins immediately noticed the difference between Joseph McTaggart and Charlie Buckingham. Unless he was good at masking his true feelings, McTaggart was nothing like his brother-in-law. Fortunately, Mrs. McTaggart hadn't fainted. She was of strong stock, and her husband seemed genuinely concerned for her welfare.

Judging by the house, the McTaggart's were more than a little comfortable. Hodgins was puzzled, though. A chemist would make a fair living in the city, not so much in a town this size. Kleinberg was just beginning to grow, and a farming community didn't generally have a lot of money to spend.

"He was getting on in years. I knew he'd pass one day. One's never fully prepared, though," Mrs. McTaggart said. "I should go see Mama. She'll need help preparing the funeral."

Hodgins shifted uncomfortably. "I'm afraid I might not have been clear. He didn't pass naturally. Someone killed him."

She leaned back in the chair. "No, not Papa. Who would want to harm him? Are you certain?"

"Yes, I'm positive. Would you like to accompany me on the afternoon train? It leaves at 2:00 p.m."

"Thank you, I'll be ready by then." She turned to her husband. "You may as well remain here and finish setting up the shop. You'll just be underfoot."

"I can't let you go on your own. I'll stay out of Charlie's way." Joseph shrugged as he turned to Hodgins. "I don't get along with my brother-in-law."

"I'll be perfectly safe. I'll have a policeman as an escort, and I'm certain Adelia will be there. That's Charlie's wife, Detective."

"Yes, I've met them both. Is there anyone either of you can think of that might wish to harm your father? It doesn't appear as if robbery was the motive. It seemed personal. Have there been any problems with the neighbours or perhaps a hired hand? Someone who was fired?"

"What about those two brothers? They didn't last long," Joseph said.

"Oh, I'd forgotten about them. They were hired to help in the fields. Mama and Papa plant a field of hay for the horses, and one of oats. They sell the oats and keep the stalks for straw. Smitty is old, like Papa, so he needed a bit of help with the planting. It was still too early to plant anything but some root vegetables, but the fields needed to be prepared, and that's work meant for younger men. Those two boys were nothing but ruffians. The older one was always waving a gun around."

"A gun? Do you know what type? How long ago was this?"

Mrs. McTaggart shrugged. "I only know what Mama told me. It was some sort of hand gun. Would have been last month."

Hodgins pulled his notebook out. "What were their names?"

"You'll have to ask Mama. I can't think of anything else to tell you. Now, if you'll excuse me, I need to pack."

After she left the room, Hodgins turned to Joseph. "Your wife is a strong woman."

"Yes, she is rather remarkable. She'll probably be crying the entire time she's packing, though. She was very close to her parents, her father in particular. I'll give her something to take in case she needs to settle her nerves."

"You mentioned you didn't get along with her brother. Any specific problems?"

"No, not really. We just don't agree on most things. Especially the way he treats his wife. Adelia is a lovely woman. Deserves better than what she got."

"How did Charlie get along with his father?"

"About as well as you'd expect. I've known the family for years. Went to school with Charlie. He was raised to treat everyone with respect, especially woman, but he never listened. I've heard more than one argument between him and Bucky."

"Bad enough to kill him? As I mentioned, it looked quite personal."

"Yes, I wondered about that. I take it he was bashed about a bit?"

"Shot through the heart, stabbed with a pitchfork, and hit on the head several times with something heavy. Haven't determined what with just yet."

"Dear God! Charlie wouldn't do something like that. Strike out in anger, yes, but all that? No, not even Charlie would stoop so low."

Hodgins tucked the notebook back into his jacket pocket. "We're all capable of murder, given the right circumstances. Some people take less provoking than others. Will you be accompanying your wife into Toronto this afternoon?"

"No. She's got quite the stubborn streak. As she said, I'll just be in the way, initially. I imagine it'll take a day or two to get everything ready." McTaggart cocked his head. "I just realized. The body won't be released for a while, I imagine. Since it was murder, and not accidental, there will be some sort of investigation."

"The coroner's done a preliminary examination, and has started looking more in depth. I imagine your father-in-law will be released today or tomorrow. I can arrange for a telegram to be sent to you."

"Thank you, Detective. I'd appreciate that. Bea should be ready to go in time to catch the train. If you wouldn't mind making sure she finds a carriage to take her to the farm?"

Hodgins nodded. "Of course. Plenty of drivers around the train station. I'll make certain she has a ride with a driver I know and trust. Some would take advantage of a woman travelling alone." Seeing the look of shock on McTaggart's face he quickly added, "Charge them double the fair, I mean."

A loud thud on the second floor startled both men. "Sounds like your wife could use a hand. I'll have a wander around town and come back about one fifteen with a buggy."

McTaggart shook his head. "No, I'll take you the station. See my wife off properly."

The walk around town didn't take long. Hodgins found an ale house not far from the McTaggart's and had an early lunch. It was mostly a working man's establishment, and they offered a Ploughman's lunch, so he decided to give it a try. The bread was fresh and still warm, and the server informed him the cheese was made just two doors down.

"I don't recall seeing a cheese shop when I walked about."

"Oh, not a proper shop. Ole Tom makes it for his family, but supplies the tavern as well. Farms don't make a lot of money, so he sells some of the cheese to make ends meet. One thing Tom's got plenty of is cows and goats. Get our milk from him and few of the other farmers. Tom's the only one who makes cheese. It's nice and sharp."

Hodgins read through his notes while nibbling on the bread and cheese. Several slices of apple accompanied the meal, the sweetness a nice compliment to the sharp tang of the cheese. When he finished, he strolled around town again, then back to the McTaggart's, arriving just after one. An average-sized travel trunk sat just outside the door, so he heaved it into the buggy that stood in front of the house before knocking. Despite the knicks and worn leather straps, the trunk didn't appear to have been used much.

Both the buggy and train rides were fairly quiet. Hodgins didn't push Beatrice for conversation as she was grieving and still in shock over the news. Her husband sat with his arm around her while Hodgins drove the buggy. When they arrived at the station, Joseph handed Hodgins a small vile of laudanum in case Beatrice needed to calm her nerves.

The train arrived back in Toronto only a little behind schedule. Hodgins found a driver he knew well, and sent Mrs. McTaggart on her way, then found another cabbie and headed to the station. Barnes, Harrington, and Riddell were back, so he rounded them up in his office.

"Ok, what've you got? Riddell?"

Riddell scowled as he flipped through his notes. "Don't like that git one little bit. Sorry, sir. Guess my personal feelings don't matter much."

"Quite all right. Didn't care much for him myself. And you should always trust your instincts. What did you learn?"

"He doesn't seem all that concerned about this father's murder. His wife's upset, and that seemed to anger him. Nothing but a bully if you ask me. Got a rather small farm, so he'd certainly gain from his father's death. Already talking about moving back and taking over. Work both farms. Since he's the only son he'll probably inherit. He mentioned a will, but hasn't seen it. He assumes it will say he gets the farm, allowing his mother to stay until she dies."

Riddell looked up. "Imagine. *Allowing* his mother to stay. Nothing but an insensitive, smarmy git. I wonder if he had a fight with his father and never made up?"

"Yes, there was mention of an issue, but I don't have any details. Might be worthwhile to try to speak with his wife when her husband isn't around. Harrington, what about the neighbour?"

"Mr. Logan. He sounds pleasant, and said he and his wife were pretty friendly with the Buckinghams. The two women chatted frequently and Mr. Logan helped out when he could. Didn't have anything good to say about the son. Even went so far as to call him a lazy son-of-a-bitch. He also hinted at a problem between Charlie and Bucky, but wouldn't elaborate. I did get the feelin' he were hiding something."

"So, neither can be fully eliminated as suspects. Could it be Logan is simply hiding something minor or rather embarrassing? Barnes, what about Mrs. Buckingham and the hired hand …"

"Smitty. He was out preparing the fields for planting so I spoke to Mrs. Buckingham first. Said she wished her husband had smoothed things over with Charlie, but didn't elaborate either. I think she wanted to, but she's still quite upset, understandably. They were married when they were eighteen. Would have been their fifty-eighth anniversary next month. Imagine being with the same person that long."

Barnes sighed. Hodgins assumed he was thinking about Violet.

"Write up your reports before you leave, then tomorrow start digging around. Talk to the neighbours, see if you can find any of Charlie's friends or old school mates. Barnes, you'll have to go back out and ask Mrs. Buckingham where Charlie and his sister went to school, who their friends were. Might be a write-up in the newspaper when they got married. See who stood with them. The daughter is Beatrice McTaggart. Came back on the train with me and went to stay with her mother. I don't believe she or her husband are involved, but see what you can find out about both of them. Husband's name is Joseph McTaggart."

He dismissed them and wrote up his own report before heading home.

* * *

Hodgins arrived home to an unusually quiet house. Sara and her two cousins sat in the parlour with the twins, taking turns helping them eat. Scraps sat beside the playpen, looking from one to the other. When they first agreed to adopt the toddlers, Hodgins wasn't sure how the dog would react to them. Scraps was very protective of his family and once he realized the little wiggling creatures were staying, he acted as their protector, too.

Any time someone came to the door, Scraps ran to the twins and sat in front of them, daring anyone to come near. Hodgins hadn't realized he wanted a larger family until Sara suggested adopting them after their natural mother had been arrested. He'd long since come to terms with having only one child after Delia lost their second and was unable to conceive again. As he watched his daughter, niece, and nephew coddling the twins, his thoughts turned to Charlie Buckingham. Hodgins hoped he'd always stay close to Sara no matter how old she was, and Holly and Ivy as well.

He walked down the hall, puzzled that no sounds came from the kitchen. Delia should be preparing their evening meal. At least the aroma of a roast filled the air. When he entered the kitchen, the table sat ready, but Delia wasn't in sight.

As soon as he heard the whirring of the sewing machine, he knew where to find her. The door to the small pantry/sewing room off the kitchen stood ajar. He pushed it open and watched as she made tiny matching dresses for the twins. A basket of wool sat on the floor beside her sewing table, several pairs of tiny socks spilling out. He coughed.

Cordelia jumped, almost falling off the chair. "Oh, you're home. I didn't hear you come in."

"Have you noticed that dog doesn't greet me as much now? Don't know if I should be insulted or glad he's taken to the twins."

She left the sewing and kissed Hodgins. "Food's ready and warming on the stove. Won't take but a minute to get it on the table. Round up the children and we can eat. Then you can tell me all about your trip to Kleinberg."

During their meal, Hodgins kept the conversation light, knowing that his brother and sister-in-law didn't like him discussing his cases in front of their children. Once the meal was over and the five kids were all in bed, Cordelia picked up her needlepoint and sat with Hodgins in the parlour.

"Elizabeth babies Freddie and Cora too much. It won't do them any harm to know that wicked people exist. Sheltering them from life does more harm than she imagines." Delia poked the needle through the fabric with more force than required.

"I agree, but it's not our decision. They have to raise them as they see fit."

Cordelia dismissed his comment with a wave of her hand. "Now, tell me everything. Do you have a suspect?"

CHAPTER FIVE

"Straight to the point as always. No, not really. So far we've turned up no evidence and no motive. The son is a heartless man, and nothing would give me more pleasure than to see him convicted for murdering his father, but I can't arrest him simply for being disagreeable."

"No evidence at all?"

"Nothing. We have the pitchfork that he was stabbed with, but it's just an ordinary farm implement. He was shot, but again, common gun. Haven't found what was used to bash his head in."

Cordelia winced. "My goodness, someone certainly wanted to make sure the poor man was dead."

Hodgins poked at the fire, trying to keep it from dying. The days were nice enough, but spring nights were still quite chilly. He added a few more logs and a bit of kindling. The low flames lapped around the small bits of wood before finally taking hold. "That should keep the room warm for a few more hours."

He wandered to the bay window, then back to his chair. He sat for a moment, then got up and paced around the room.

"What's troubling you, Bertie?"

"People are keeping secrets. I just don't like it. I know most folks don't like to air their dirty laundry, especially to the police, but a man's been murdered, damn it. A helpless, seventy-six-year-old man. It was a horrible sight. Almost puked when I saw him."

Finally, he sat back down onto the chair opposite Cordelia. Exhaustion took hold and he slumped.

"I'm worn out, Delia. Frustrated and completely disheartened with my fellow man. Do you have any good news? Something to cheer me up?"

"Well, I have two pieces of news; something you already know, but one thing I suspect you don't. You are aware that Henry's sweetheart, Violet, is returning shortly?"

Hodgins nodded. "The lad's been in quite a state. One minute he's happy, next he's convinced she's coming back either engaged or married."

Cordelia smiled. "There is a gentleman coming back with them, which you know, but it's not that nobleman. And he's betrothed to her aunt. Imagine, becoming engaged at her age."

Hodgins smiled. "Barnes will be very happy to hear that. He'll probably still moan about how she's outgrown him, though. How old is Halloway's sister? Must be in her mid-fortes. First marriage? Who'd she hook?"

"Bertie, really. Hook indeed. You met her before they left. She's quite nice, and very attractive. I don't know much, but Mrs. Halloway mentioned he's a businessman. Must be doing quite well to need to travel to Europe. You'll meet him soon enough. Two days after they arrive, the Halloways are throwing a big party to officially announce their engagement. She hinted the marriage will take place soon."

She waggled a finger at him when he grinned. "And no, they don't *have* to get married."

Hodgins held his hands up. "I never said a word. Maybe they can have a double wedding. Put Henry out of his misery once and for all."

He stifled a yawn and rose. "I think I'd best be

heading to bed. I want to go out to the Buckingham's farm and poke about some more. The killer must have left some clues behind. And maybe I can coerce the widow to tell me what the problem was between her husband and son. Barnes said he felt she wanted to tell him, but was still in shock."

Delia stood with him and kissed his cheek. "You go up. I want to finish the little dresses for Holly and Ivy. I think it's time the community finally met them, and I'd like to dress them up for church. I know people have been talking about us taking them in, but I don't care. They're not responsible for what their mother did. Once everyone sees how sweet they are, I'm certain the tongues will stop wagging. Most of them, anyway."

"Ever the optimist, dear. Don't stay up too late."

* * *

Next morning, Hodgins rose before Cordelia and re-lit the fire in the bedroom. He hadn't even noticed when she came to bed. Careful not to wake her, he made certain to avoid the squeaky step when he went downstairs. Before taking Scraps for a quick walk, he started a fire in the stove. The house wasn't too cold, so the rest of the fires didn't need to be lit.

He took the dog over to the park beside Ketchum School to let him have a good run. Unfortunately, Scraps found the only mud puddle on the property and rolled in it until everything except his eyes were filthy.

The mud. Hodgins pulled his notebook from his jacket and made a note to check the farm for footprints as soon as possible. It had rained off and on for the past week. Maybe there were prints around the barn they'd missed, assuming they hadn't been trampled over. He needed to find something. Anything. If even one print didn't fit anyone on the farm, or his constables, it could help narrow down their suspects.

When they returned home, Cordelia was up and preparing breakfast. Hodgins kept the dog in the back porch until he rubbed most of the mud off. When he opened the door to the house, Scraps went straight to his bowl and sat. Hodgins fed him, then made a cup of tea for both himself and Cordelia. It had been too long since they'd enjoyed a quiet breakfast together.

He nodded towards Scraps. "He gave me a hint this morning, rolling around in the mud. I need check something at the Buckingham place. See if there are any prints in the mud that can't be identified."

They both looked up at the ceiling when they heard running.

"The children are up. That means the twins will be awake and wailing to be fed soon."

Cordelia started to rise, but Hodgins touched her arm. "Stay. I'll get the twins and bring them down."

Before going up, he filled two bottles with milk and set them in a pot of water on the stove. When he came back down, Cordelia had removed them from the fire and had mashed up some carrots.

Sara, Cora, and Freddie watched as Delia helped Holly eat. Hodgins sat with Ivy on his lap. She devoured her portion of mushy carrots and guzzled all her milk.

* * *

Hodgins arrived at Station Number Four long before any of the constables who were helping him. He dug their reports out of the filing cabinet and spread them across an empty table. One thing remained consistent with every report. Each constable had the feeling the person they'd interviewed was hiding something, but what? Were they all hiding the same thing, or were there three different secrets? Somehow, he had to find out. One of those secrets could be the reason someone wanted Bucky dead.

The dog's muddy paws triggered a foggy memory. Hodgins read through the constable's reports, then his own. He snapped his fingers. The overalls and boots in one of the empty stalls. The rubber boots were muddy. He tried to get a clear picture in his mind. The boots were relatively small. He recalled that much. At the time he'd thought they wouldn't fit him. Not small enough to belong to a woman though. A man of slight build possibly?

Images of the family and neighbour swirled around his mind. The son wasn't a terribly large man. Neither was the son-in-law. Hodgins made a mental note to inquire further about the hired hand. He still hadn't met him and neither had any of the constables. They had no clue what he looked like.

The detective cursed and went back through the reports, just in case he'd missed something. None of the constables had spoken to the hired hand, Smitty. He always seemed to be out in the field. Was it just a matter of bad timing, or was he trying to hide? Hodgins checked the time. If he left now, maybe he could get to the farm before the man arrived.

He rushed to John Mitchell's livery and hired a small, one-horse shay and headed out to the Buckingham farm. If Smitty arrived first, he'd be out in one of the fields. Again. Hodgins didn't look forward to tromping through acres of semi-muddy farmland trying to locate him. The grey pony foamed around the bridle from being pushed so hard. When he arrived, the widow and her daughter were finishing up the breakfast dishes.

"Good morning, Mrs. McTaggart. Sorry to disturb you so early, but I was hoping to speak with the hired hand before he started work."

"Come into the kitchen, Detective. I'm sorry, but you've made the trip for naught. Smitty sent a note saying he was ill and wouldn't be able to work for a few days."

"Sent a note?"

"Yes. It's the most peculiar thing. He paid a cabbie to deliver it. He's never been one to spend money without good reason."

Hodgins took his notebook from his jacket and

fished around for his stubby pencil. "May I?" He indicated towards one of the kitchen chairs.

"Yes, by all means. Would you like a cup of tea? It's still rather chilly."

"That would be most welcome, thank you. Can I assume that Smitty doesn't live on the property?"

"He has a room near the eastern edge of the city. If he works too late, he'll sleep in the barn loft. I do wish he'd stay permanently," Mrs. Buckingham said. "Smitty's almost seventy. I've never liked him making the trip back into the city at night. Walks you know. He's still quite spry, but a man his age shouldn't be working, especially hard as he does."

Hodgins poised his pencil over a blank page. "What can you tell me about him? Where can I find the room he rents? Does he have any family?"

"I have the address written down. It's somewhere in the desk." Mrs. Buckingham started to rise, but her daughter stopped her.

"Sit, Mama. I'll find it. You tell the detective what you know about Smitty."

As Mrs. McTaggart left the room, Mrs. Buckingham dabbed at her eyes with a handkerchief.

"Don't know what I'd do without Beatrice. We've always been close, but she was especially close to her father. He was heartbroken when they decided to move to Kleinberg."

Hodgins gave her a minute to compose herself, then prompted her again. "Smitty?"

"Quiet man. Never spoke much about himself and we never pried. There was that one night, though. A couple of years ago we had an exceptionally good crop. Not too wet, not too dry. Had more than enough hay and straw to get us through the winter. Extra oats too. Sold all the excess and had pretty penny to put in the bank. Bucky and Smitty celebrated.

"When Bucky took the money to the bank, he stopped to visit an old friend at Gooderham and Worts and brought home a bottle of their whisky. Him and Smitty dang near finished the bottle. I was trying to get them to go to bed and sleep it off when Smitty muttered something about me nagging him like his wife. I asked him about it next day, but he just shook his head and went into the fields."

Hodgins made a few notes. "So, you don't know for certain whether or not he was married?"

Beatrice returned with a scrap of paper and showed it to her mother. "Is this his address?"

"Yes, that's the place."

Beatrice handed it to Hodgins, who then copied it into his notebook. "Is Smitty a small man? Can you describe him please?"

"Small? Heavens no. He's tall. Plenty of meat on his bones. The man certainly enjoys his meals. Not fat, mind you. And he's rather strong, for a man his age that is."

Hodgins closed his notebook. "Would you mind if I looked around the farm a bit? Just in case we missed something the other day."

"Anything that will help find who killed my father," Beatrice said. "Have you any word when his body will be released?"

"I'll check with the coroner when I return to the city. Would you like him brought out here or will he be laid to rest in the city?"

"He'll be buried here, on the farm."

"I'll make sure he's brought over as soon as the coroner releases him. Just one more question, Mrs. Buckingham. Can you tell me what your husband and son argued about?"

"Argument? Which one? You know children. Always disagreeing with their parents about something and nothing, no matter how old they get. If you'll excuse me, I am rather tired."

"Of course." Hodgins made a note of how she looked away as soon as he asked about the argument, but he didn't want to push her so soon after the murder. He closed his notebook and stood. "Thank you for the tea. I'll try not to disturb you any further."

Hodgins went back to the barn to check the rubber boots. The area where the body had been found was completely cleaned up. The straw had been swept, and the floor boards scrubbed clean. Both horses stood in their stalls, quietly munching on hay. He went into the empty stall where he'd seen the overalls and boots. Both were still there. Hodgins picked up one of the boots and set it beside his foot. It was almost two inches shorter than his. The mud that clung to the bottom flaked when he picked them up. No way to tell when they'd last been worn. He thought back. The mud had been shiny, fresh. Those boots had been worn recently, possibly the day of the murder. He put the boot back and walked around the exterior of the barn.

A few puddles still speckled the property. It hadn't been warm enough to completely dry them up and Hodgins found a small semi-dried puddle beside an exit at the back of the barn. One solitary footprint had been left when the puddle started to dry. Hodgins carefully stepped around it and tried the door. It was unlocked. He went in, retrieved the left boot, and took it back to the puddle. Gently he lowered the boot into the print. It fit perfectly.

Hodgins went back inside the barn, picked up the other boot, then placed the pair on the floor of the shay before going back to the house.

"Sorry to disturb you again, but I have a question. Whose boots are those in the barn? They belong to someone with feet a little smaller than mine."

Mrs. McTaggart glanced down at Hodgins feet. "I'm sorry, but I don't know. Papa was about your size, and Smitty is quite a bit larger. Mama has tiny feet, and I saw her boots in the mud porch. She wears them in the vegetable garden out back. I can't think who else would have left them."

"I'll be taking them to the station. They match a print I found behind the barn. Please try to stay away from it. I'll send a photographer out to take a picture of it and leave instructions for him not to disturb you."

Her eyes went wide. "Do you think it was left by the person who killed Papa? Why would he have left his boots in the barn?"

"I can't answer that, but it's the only lead we have. The photographer should be out later this morning. Good day, ma'am."

* * *

Hodgins took the boots back to the station, had Barnes lock them away and arrange for the photographer, then went to the address for Smitty. Unfortunately, he wasn't there and the landlady didn't know where he'd gone.

"Paid up for the week and left. Don't know nothing else. You're welcome ta look in his room, but be quick about it. Need ta clean it up and rent it out right quick."

CHAPTER SIX

It didn't take long for Hodgins to look through the room. One bed against a wall, a small table and chair sat under a dirty window, with a wardrobe tucked into the corner. He found nothing under the bed. The wardrobe contained two empty wire hangers, and the drawer in the desk had one empty whisky bottle. The landlady stood in the doorway the entire time.

"Did he ever mention his family? Maybe say where he was headed?"

"Tol' ya. Don't know nothin'. Man weren't one for chatter. Left early, came in late, kept to 'imself."

"What direction did he go when he left?"

"West."

Hodgins knew he wasn't going to get any useful information from her. He tipped his homburg. "Thank you for your time."

West. Hodgins stood outside the boarding house

at the corner of Glen and Howard. Where could he be going? The only thing that came to mind was the train. If Smitty regularly walked from the farm to the boarding house, he wouldn't have a problem walking to the train. Not feeling particularly energetic, Hodgins walked over to Sherbourne and waited for the trolley to take him down to Front Street.

Finally, Hodgins caught a break. The ticket agent remembered a tall, husky, elderly man.

"He bought a ticket for Collingwood. Said there was a family emergency and begged to be allowed to ride the mail train that was just about ready to leave. It left right on time. Twenty minutes to eight this morning. Should arrive 'bout one."

"Damn. When's the next train?"

"Shortly after one this afternoon. Would you like a ticket?"

"Not right now, thank you."

Hodgins hailed a hansom cab rather than wait for a streetcar to take him to the station house. When he walked through the front door he called to Barnes. "Office."

Barnes picked up his notebook and hurried into

the detective's office.

"How'd you like to take a trip up north with me? That blasted hired hand has scarpered off. Took the morning train to Collingwood. Next one leaves in two hours. Head home and pack a bag."

"Overnight? Violet will be coming home tomorrow."

"Sorry, but police business comes first. If you're going to marry her, she'll have to learn that a police officer has horrible hours. You'll have plenty of time with her when we return."

Barnes' shoulders dropped. "Yes, sir."

"Don't fret lad. I'll ask Cordelia to let the Halloways know. With any luck, we only have to spend one day there."

Hodgins pulled out his pocket watch. "No time to dawdle. We'd best get our satchels. Meet me at Union Station right quick."

* * *

Barnes stood at the entrance to the station when Hodgins arrived, train tickets in hand. "Ma packed some food." Barnes held up a small sack. "Said the food on the train isn't very good."

Hodgins laughed. "Cordelia said much the same thing. We won't go hungry, that's for certain. I think we'll have enough for lunch and supper. I stopped at the station and grabbed all the reports. We can review them along the way."

"Do you think the hired hand killed Mr. Buckingham? Don't normally come across old men killing people."

"I don't know what to think. There's the train now. Let's settle in then I'll tell you what I discovered this morning."

They found a spot in the back corner of the passenger car and Hodgins spread the reports on the seat beside him.

"I went back to the farm early before coming in, hoping to finally speak with Smitty. After finding out he sent word he was ill, I looked around the barn some more. A pair of rubber boots stood in one of the empty stalls, fresh mud on them when I spotted them yesterday. Walked around the barn and found a footprint in a partially dried mud puddle by a back entrance. Fit the boot perfectly."

"That'd be the boots you brought in."

"Right. Went to the boarding house where Smitty stayed and found out he paid his rent and left. Only thing in the room was an empty whisky bottle. I took a chance he came to the train station, and found out he'd bought a ticket to Collingwood, and here we are, following him."

"Looks mighty guilty, if you ask me. But why would he kill his employer? From what I learned when I went back, they got along fine."

"Secrets, Barnes. Everyone seems to have secrets. Found out this morning that Smitty mentioned a wife once when drunk. The widow didn't know if he was making a general comment or referring to his wife. No one seems to know anything at all about him. What's up in Collingwood? If he was on the run, surely he'd go farther. South across the border possibly. I can't help but wonder if he has family up there. Not a place an old man would go looking for work."

Barnes settled back as the train started to move, the hiss of the steam drowning his words. He leaned forward and tried again. "I said, did you find out why the son disliked his father?"

"Blast," Hodgins said. "I should have left

instructions for Harrington and Riddell." He pulled the train schedule out of his satchel.

"Wonder if the stop at Allendale will be for long? It's a changeover for people taking the Muskoka line. If there's time, I can send a telegram."

"We've been talking it over, sir. We're all anxious to catch the killer. Riddell wants to speak with the son and neighbour again, and Harrington has already started looking into school chums. They'll keep busy while we're away."

"I'm sure you're right. I would like someone to look into McTaggart's business in Toronto. Can't for the life of me imagine why he'd leave the city to set up in a hamlet so far north. Just doesn't make sense. I honestly don't believe either of the McTaggarts had anything to do with it, but there's got to be something they aren't telling me."

The train arrived in Collingwood just after 5:30 p.m. Neither Hodgins nor Barnes expected quite so many people to be about.

"Gosh," Barnes said. "I never imagined this many people were up here. Smells about the same as Toronto, but not quite. Strong smell of fish, what with the water being right there." Barnes pointed to the bay. "Doesn't smell as dirty, though."

"Not quite so many factories. Keeps the air a little fresher. Even the fish don't have the same pungent odour. First thing, I'll check with the station master and see if he recalls seeing Smitty, then we'll find a place to stay the night. Wait here."

Five minutes later Hodgins returned. "Smitty got off the train when it arrived at one. Seems he's originally from these parts. The station master was surprised he was back, but didn't elaborate. Doesn't know where he went, but said Smitty still has family in town. Daughter's married to someone by the name of Coffey who works at the ship builders, Holman, Watts, & Co. Suppose that's as good a place to start as any, but it can wait until morning. The agent suggested we stay at the Globe Hotel. It's not far. I'll book our rooms then we can find something to eat. All that food we ate on the train and I'm still peckish."

* * *

First thing next morning, Hodgins and Barnes went over to the ship builders to speak with Smitty's son-in-law, Archibald Coffey. They arrived just before the shift started and were only able to speak with him for a few moments.

"Yes, he's back. Just turned up at our door. Never thought that old bugger'd dare show his face again."

"And why is that, Mr. Coffey? Didn't get along with your father-in-law?" Hodgins nodded to Barnes, indicating he should take notes.

"Not that. Pleasant enough bloke. When sober, that is. Suppose you'll find out eventually. His wife died under peculiar circumstances. Smitty'd been at the Central Hotel, drinking. Came home and had a row with his wife. My wife, Myrtle, had been visiting. We'd only just got married a few months earlier. Told her Pa to get out, and he did. Myrtle stayed a bit, then came home and told me about it. Next day, she went back to see how her Ma was. Found her dead. Had a black eye, head cracked open on the hearth. No one's seen Smitty since, 'til yesterday."

Hodgins looked over at Barnes, who hastily wrote in his little notebook. He waited until the constable caught up, then returned his attention to Coffey.

"Well, that seems to be one secret uncovered. Would you object if we spoke with your wife?"

Coffey shrugged. "Fine with me. She'll be home, tending the wee one." A huge grin spread across his face. "First grandchild. A boy. Our Maggie married the tailor last year."

Barnes wrote down the address Coffey provided, then they followed the directions, straight to a pretty little cottage. Not large, but big enough for the Coffey's and their daughter's family. As they approached the front door, the familiar sounds of a cooing baby reached the detective's ears. A young lady, in her early or mid-twenties, opened the door. Hodgins introduced himself and Barnes, and she stepped back to allow them entry.

"Is your mother about? I'd like to speak with her, if it's convenient."

Maggie gave Hodgins a puzzled looked, but called for her mother. Mrs. Coffey came out of a room to the left, carrying an infant.

"Detective up from Toronto wants to speak with you, Ma."

"It's about your father," Hodgins said.

"What's that man done now?" Mrs. Coffey asked.

Barnes already had his notebook and pencil ready.

Hodgins smiled. He looked back at Mrs. Coffey.

"Nothing, at least not that we're certain of. Is he here?"

"No. He may be my father, but he's never acted like it. He killed Ma, then disappeared. The gall of that man to show up unannounced. Told him to leave, just like I did all those years ago. Fortunately, this time he didn't come back."

"If he does, please send word. We're staying at the Globe."

On their way back to the hotel, shouting merged with the waves slapping against the rocky shoreline. Men ran towards the lake. Hodgins stopped one of them and asked what had happened.

"Body washed up on shore."

CHAPTER SEVEN

Hodgins and Barnes followed the crowd to the shore of Georgian Bay. Two men pulled a body out of the water and flipped him on his back.

"Who is it?" someone hollered.

"Don't recognize him," replied one of the men who pulled him out. "Old man. Not a local."

Hodgins and Barnes pushed their way through the growing crowd. "Toronto Constabulary."

The men moved back, but quickly returned, wanting to get a look at the corpse. The drowned man was tall and rather large. Hodgins looked at Barnes. "Fits Smitty's description. Run to the ship builders and get Coffey."

Barnes took off and the questions started.

"Who's Smitty?"

"Why's a copper up from Toronto?"

"Was he a dangerous criminal?"

Hodgins tried to get the crowd to stay back from the body. "Is there a doctor in town?"

Several people murmured *yes*.

"You." Hodgins pointed at the man closest to him. "Go find him."

"Ain't nothing a doctor can do for that poor sot now."

"Just go find him. Now!"

The man shrugged and slowly made his way into town. Hodgins examined the body as best he could, looking for any signs of foul play. A boy came running along the shore, yelling.

"Busted up boat in the rocks."

He stopped when he saw the dead body. "He the man from the boat?"

"Might be." Hodgins turned towards the crowd.

"Did anyone see anything? Hear anybody yelling for help?"

"Can't hear much anything with the water crashing up along the rocks. Water was a little choppy last night. Anyone who'd take a boat out was a fool."

Heads nodded in agreement.

Barnes finally returned with Coffey, who stood

over the body, examining the face.

"Looks like him. Can't say I'm sorry to see he's dead. Wife'll be glad to hear the news. Can I get back to work now?"

"Don't you want to tell your wife?" Barnes asked.

"Boss'll have my hide if I'm away much longer. You can give her the good news yourself, Constable."

Without waiting for an answer, Coffey turned and headed back to the ship builders. The men in the crowd started talking at once. One called out after Coffey.

"Hey Archie. Someone you know?"

Without stopping or turning around, Coffey answered. "No account father-in-law."

The man Hodgins sent after the doctor returned as Coffey left. Hodgins introduced himself to the physician.

"A detective, eh? Don't see many of those up here." He extended his hand. "Dr. Moberly. Doesn't look like this man is in need of my services."

"Habits from the city," Hodgins replied. "I always call the coroner before moving the body. Thought you could have a quick look. Confirm drowning and not foul play. Mr. Smith wasn't popular around here years ago. Someone could still hold a grudge."

"Be glad to. It's been rather slow today. Good excuse to get out and enjoy the nice weather."

Moberly knelt down beside the body and checked him over. "No blood or wounds that appear unusual that I can see. That mark on his temple there? Seen that plenty of times when people bash their heads on the rocks. Sometimes fatal, sometimes not. It's not deep. If he was in the water, then he may have been knocked unconscious and simply drowned. I don't see anything that looks suspicious, so I doubt there'll be an investigation. Happens all the time. Did I hear correctly? This is Mr. Coffey's father-in-law? I grew up with Archie's daughter, Maggie. I've heard rumours about her grandfather."

"Yes, I've heard them too. Don't imagine we'll ever know for certain now. I'll need to have Mrs. Coffey confirm this is her father. Is there somewhere you can take his body?"

"Yes. Since I walked up, someone will have to bring him to my office. He can go to the cemetery from there. I imagine he'll be buried in the Anglican church beside his wife. Not certain there'll be many in attendance."

One of the men in the crowd volunteered his wagon to transport the body, and the crowed eventually disbursed. Hodgins and Barnes made the trek to the Coffey residence to relay the news and ask Mrs. Coffey to go to the doctor's to positively identify her father's body.

"Do you think he planned to die?" Barnes asked as they made their way back to the hotel.

"Don't suppose we'll ever know. May as well go back to the hotel and collect our things. We've plenty of time to grab a bite and still make the 1:10 p.m. train back to Toronto. Nothing more we can do here now. At least we've learned one of the secrets."

"We'll be back in time to meet the ship. Violet's due in tonight."

"Yes, Barnes, I know. You've spoken of nothing else for weeks. Party Saturday evening, I understand. And I happen to know Violet's not coming home married, or with a new beau. What time is the ship expected to dock?"

"If it's on schedule, around seven tonight."

"That's less than ten minutes before the train's due

to pull in to Union. You won't have time to go home and freshen up. If the train and ship are both on time, we can wait and take one carriage."

"I'd like to send Ma a telegram, if you don't mind. Let her know I'll be home tonight but won't have time for supper."

Hodgins slapped Barnes on the back. "By all means, lad. And don't waste any more time before you ask that girl to marry you."

* * *

The train arrived back in Toronto right on schedule. Hodgins had telegrammed ahead for a carriage to pick them up. They scrambled in and headed to the port to wait for the ship.

"It's running late," the harbour master said. "Bit of bad weather on the way, but she'll be here by 8:30 tonight."

Hodgins turned to Barnes. "Why don't you go home and freshen up, then wait at the Halloway's, or with my family. The ship won't arrive any quicker with you hanging about the docks."

"Well, I suppose that might be best. Put on a fresh shirt."

"I'll tell the driver to wait for the ship and pay him for his time. Save them the bother of finding a cabbie at night. We can take the trolley."

* * *

Hodgins arrived home to the surprise of Cordelia. Unlike Barnes, he hadn't bothered to send her a telegram. Scraps raced down the hall and leapt up as soon as Hodgins entered. Sara was in the parlour watching the twins stumble as they waddled, Cordelia keeping a close eye on them. Holly started walking months ago, but Ivy hadn't quite got the hang of it.

"Bertie, I didn't expect you for another day. Was the trip successful?"

"Yes and no." He ruffled Sara's hair before joining his wife on the settee.

"Mr. Smith, Smitty, was in Collingwood, but we didn't get the chance to speak with him. He'd stopped at his daughter's but she sent him away. Blames him for the death of her mother. His body washed up on shore early this morning. I don't believe he's guilty of killing Mr. Buckingham, and we'll never know if his wife's death was murder. He may have accidentally drowned, or possibly took a boat out in the bay in bad weather on purpose. There was nothing left for us to do up there, so we came home. Barnes is quite happy. Getting cleaned up then going to wait for Violet to arrive home. The ship's late due to bad weather."

"Drowned himself in the bay? How horrible. Why would he even think of doing such a thing?"

"Don't know the whole story, but he was suspected of killing his wife while drunk. No evidence to provide it wasn't an accident, but if he drowned himself, maybe he did do it."

"If he could have killed his wife, why rule him out for the murder of his employer"?

Hodgins took Delia's hand. "Smitty was an old man. He wouldn't have had the strength to drive a pitchfork through the body. Now, can we speak of more pleasant things? How were the twins? I missed them more than I imagined."

"Oh, they've been ever so good, Daddy." Sara held Ivy's hand. "Look, she's finally started to take several steps all on her own. Well, almost on her own."

Sara slowly guided Ivy towards her parents. After only four steps, the toddler fell on her bottom. She looked as though about to cry, but Sara's laugh brightened her, and she clapped her tiny hands and laughed too.

"I suppose one day we'll have to consider how to tell them about their parents," Delia said. "How does one tell a child her mother was responsible for the death of their father? Have you caught the murderer yet?"

Hodgins leaned back and closed his eyes. "We sent the description Mrs. Brown gave us of the man she hired to all the police stations within two hundred miles, both sides of the border. Got something from the Buffalo police. A man matching his description killed someone in a brawl outside a tavern. Several witnesses, so there's no doubt he's guilty of that crime. We can't prove he's the man she hired, so when they asked if we wanted him up here to prosecute, I told them no. Let them pay to have him hung."

He took a whiff of the air. "I suppose I've missed supper? Didn't have a thing to eat on the train."

Cordelia shrugged. "I wasn't expecting you back today, so I didn't bother preparing anything elaborate. We just had cold roast beef. Yesterday's leftovers."

"My dear, your cold leftovers are highly superior to

anything they serve on the train. I trust you have biscuits or scones to go with it? And some of your peach preserves?"

* * *

Next morning, Barnes arrived at the station a half hour after Hodgins. For the first time since Christmas, the constable smiled. He even whistled when he walked through the front door.

Hodgins called him into his office. "Might one assume all went well with your reunion?"

"Oh yes. Quite well. She and her aunt did come back with a bachelor, but he's betrothed to Aunt Bridget. The party Saturday isn't a welcome home, but an engagement party. Mr. Halloway has given his approval, so they'll be married in a few weeks, then go back to France to live. Imagine. Living in France. His business in Europe is doing so well, he moved permanently. He has a vineyard just outside Paris."

"Maybe you can visit them for your honeymoon. Have you popped the question yet?"

Barnes shook his head. "Every time I plan to, something with this murder comes up. Maybe I can sneak her off during her aunt's engagement party and ask."

"Not sure that's a good idea. Her aunt might not want her party usurped with the news of Violet's engagement. Women can be funny that way."

"Men too, I think," Barnes replied.

"You're right there. Have you asked her father for her hand? Or is that too old fashioned? Do young men still do that?"

Barnes cocked his head. "I hadn't thought of that. I suppose I should. Would it be out of place to ask him at the party? He wouldn't say anything to take away from Aunt Bridget's moment."

"Excellent idea. He'll be chuffed, I'm sure. Then you can ask Violet Sunday."

"Maybe I'll do that before church. We can ask the victor to announce it to everyone." Barnes mood improved noticeably.

"About time, too. Does this mean you can finally give your full attention to the job at hand?"

Barnes turned a light shade of pink. "Sorry, sir. I guess I have been somewhat distracted these past few months. Won't happen again."

Hodgins spotted Constables Riddell and

Harrington entering the station house. "Barnes, fetch them in here, and have them bring any notes they have. I want to find out what they were up to while we were away."

Ten minutes later, Riddell, Harrington, and Barnes crowded into Hodgins office, papers in hand. Riddell went first.

"I went back to the son's farm, Charlie Buckingham. He was out so I was able to speak to his wife. Found out why he and his father weren't on good terms. Disagreement about how to run the farm. Charlie wanted to modernize it, hire help younger than that old codger, Smith." He looked up from his notes. "She said those were her husband's words. Said Charlie didn't trust him, that he drank too much, and took too long to tend to the fields."

"Well, he was right about one thing," Hodgins said. "Smith did drink too much. He's dead now, drowned. Anything else?"

"Yes, sir. I tracked down a few of Charlie's old school mates. No one had anything good to say about him. Charlie was stand-off-ish, thought he was superior, smarter. They all agreed he was smart, but he treated everyone as though they were inferior. Not one could name any close friends he had. Even said the only reason Charlie got married was because Adelia's father caught them in the barn and forced the marriage for the sake of his daughter's reputation."

"That all?"

"Seems he has a bad temper, not above raising his fists." Riddell closed his notebook.

"Very good. Harrington? What have you discovered?"

"Not very much, I'm afraid." He didn't bother checking his notes. "I'm positive Logan is hiding something, but I haven't found out what. He did make a comment about one of the Buckingham's fields, but wouldn't elaborate."

"Could be something there. Check the land records. Never know what you might find. Keep digging and see what turns up."

Hodgins dismissed them but held Barnes back. "I think it's time to have another chat with the widow and her daughter. Why don't you come with me? Check around the property again while I see if I can get any more information."

They hired a buggy from the livery and headed east across The Don. Twenty minutes later Hodgins and Barnes climbed down from the buggy and headed up the porch stairs.

Mr. McTaggart looked surprised when he opened the door. "Good morning, Detective. Please, come in. Have you found anything new?"

"Discovered a few things here and there. Would you mind if my constable had another look around the farm? Just in case we missed something."

"Of course. Anything to help."

Barnes wandered off to check the property again and Hodgins joined the family in the parlour. Mrs. Buckingham looked a little better than on his first visit, but still visibly distraught. Hodgins imagined after being married so long, she was bound to be at a loss. Her entire routine forever changed.

"I hate to bring bad news, but I found Mr. Smith. Unfortunately, he drowned yesterday. I truly believe he wasn't involved in Mr. Buckingham's death, due to his age and lack of physical strength. You mentioned a couple of lads that worked here briefly. What can you tell me about them?"

"They were only here for a few days. I can't imagine they'd have done anything to my father," Mrs. McTaggart said. "Mother barely mentioned them."

"They were brothers," Mrs. Buckingham said. "Biblical names. Let me think. The older one was James."

She paused, trying to recall the other. "Peter. That's it. James and Peter. James was always playing with his pistol. Wonder he never shot anything, waving it about so."

"Mother, you never mentioned that."

"They were only here two or three days. Didn't want to bother you with it."

"Waving a pistol around? Interesting. There was a fellow shooting a pistol in town just the other day."

Hodgins made a note in his book, wondering if it was a coincidence that two young men were being reckless with a gun.

"Can you give me a description of the brothers?" Hodgins poised his pencil, waiting for the information.

"I'd say they were in their early to mid-twenties. Not much older. Slight, but not skinny. Seemed to have strong arms. And one of them had a funny little mole."

"What about hair colour?"

"Black, rather unkempt. Nice looking lads, but quite lazy I'm afraid. Actually came back asking to be re-hired."

Hodgins cocked his head and stared at the corner of the room, trying to recall something. *The mole.*

"How long ago did they return, Mrs. Buckingham?"

"Oh, just a few days ago, maybe a week. Is that important?"

"Could be. Do you recall their surname?"

"Bucky may have known, or Smitty. I don't bother with such things. The farm help was dealt with by my husband. The brothers weren't here long enough to have written down their names and address."

"What about your son? Would he know?"

Mrs. Buckingham shrugged.

Disappointed, Hodgins put his notebook back in his pocket.

"Thank you for your time. I'll see if my constable has found anything."

CHAPTER EIGHT

Hodgins stood on the front porch, looking around at the large farm property. Whatever was used to bash the poor man's head in had to be around somewhere. He couldn't imagine anyone taking something covered in blood with him.

His mind wandered, trying to picture the person who could have killed Bucky. If he had been shot first, it wouldn't have required much strength to weld an object and hit an old man who was already on the ground, quite possibly already dead. He shook his head. No, not a woman. It would be quite unusual for a woman to kill a man in such a manner. Poison probably, gun maybe, but to then stab him with a pitchfork and batter him about the head? No, most likely a man. An angry one.

He spotted Barnes coming from the outhouse and walked out to meet him.

"Long shot, but I thought maybe the killer might have dropped something down the hole. Fortunately, I couldn't spot anything out of the ordinary. Wouldn't want to be the one having to retrieve it."

Hodgins laughed. "Nor I, lad. So can I assume you haven't found anything?"

"Nothing. The muddy footprint you found behind the barn is almost dry now. Not sure how that will help us any."

"If we can find the person who fits the boots and had access to the farm, it might point to the killer, or at least a witness. The print was probably made around the time Buckingham was killed. May as well head back to the station. I want to look at the report about the young man waving the gun around the other day. Those two brothers that were fired, one of them had a mole, and I seem to recall the idiot waving the gun had one, too. Before we go back, I need to pay a visit to Charlie. See if he knows the last name of the two brothers."

* * *

Charlie Buckingham saddled up a horse as they arrived. He was not in a good mood.

"Make it quick. Some of the cattle didn't return last night and I've got to go find them. Hope those damn coyotes ain't been around again. Damn near lost a pregnant cow few weeks back, just about ready to calf. Fortunately, the donkey made short work of the coyote, and both the cow and calf survived. Got red Shorthorns. Great beef cattle. Now, what do you want?"

"Do you happen to know the names of the two brothers your father fired?"

"Clerk or Clark. Something like that. Is that everything?"

"Yes, that's all I needed. Good luck finding your missing cattle."

Charlie grunted and went back to saddling the horse.

On the ride back, Barnes filled Hodgins in on his reunion with Violet, and the future husband of her aunt.

"He's quite well off, it seems. They met him at the Louvre and, according to Violet, he just tagged along with them. He and Aunt Bridget seemed to have the same opinion about most of the artwork. Invited them to dinner that very evening. He showed them all over Paris, and they corresponded during the rest of their European tour. They went back to Paris for another week, and he proposed. What is it they call that? A whirlwind romance?"

"Yes, that sounds about right. I suppose at their age, they don't have time to lollygag like you young folks. Miss. Halloway is in her mid-forties after all. Probably thought she'd never wed. I image Violet must feel the say way." Hodgins grinned and winked at Barnes.

"No more lollygagging, sir. I told you, Sunday I ask for her hand. Assuming her father gives permission Saturday."

"I'm certain he will. Maybe you can do that as soon as you arrive Saturday. She'll most likely still be getting ready for the party and you can talk to him while you wait. I know he's fond of you and I can't image he'll object. Shame her aunt will be in Paris and won't be able to attend the wedding, unless …"

"Sir?"

"I was just saying to Cordelia it would be something if you could have a double wedding.

Assuming the ladies don't object. They can be quite fussy about being the centre of attention."

"Why, that's a fabulous idea. I'm sure Violet won't object. She's quite close to Aunt Bridget and would want her at the wedding."

Hodgins grinned, glad to hear Henry speaking positively for a change. No more moaning about how Violet outgrew him while in Europe.

"Then I'll expect an announcement at church Sunday. Delia will want to throw a party. Mrs. Halloway will be busy with Bridget's arrangements, so they'll probably be glad to have Delia lend a hand arranging a second party and the expanding wedding."

They returned the buggy to the livery and Barnes retrieved the file on the street shooting as soon as he entered the station house. He joined Hodgins in his office.

"Here is it. Not much information." Barnes pulled the single sheet of paper from the folder. "No one knew who the lad was."

He put the paper on the desk so Hodgins could look at it, and pointed to one line, mid-way down the page.

"Here. One witness said he noticed a mole on the gunman's ear. Did Mrs. Buckingham say where the mole was?"

"No. Just said it was a funny little mole. Go find the man who gave this report and ask him if he can describe the mole any further. See if he calls it being funny looking as well. I'll ask around see if anyone knows of two brothers, one with a mole. I hope Charlie was correct with the name. Clerk or Clark. Common names, but if they took work on a farm, maybe someone at the livery or granary might know them." Hodgins flipped through his notebook looking for the names. "Here, James and Peter. It's not much but it's better than nothing."

Barnes headed to the address listed for the person who got the best look at the young man waving the gun around, and Hodgins pulled out the City Directory for the addresses of any business where a labourer might look for work. Most were near the waterfront for easy access to the railway and shipyard.

As his investigation took him downtown, Hodgins stopped in at Paterson & Son on King Street and Rodden & Son on Bay Street as they both dealt with agriculture implements. No one had heard of the brothers or recognized their description. Hodgins made his way down to the Western Cattle Market, unsure if he was even looking in the right places. Just because the brothers tried their hand at farming, didn't mean they had any experience in anything related to agriculture.

The smell of manure and urine hit hard as soon as he went in. Soft mooing drifted from another section. At least it wasn't as bad as the abattoir. He'd not eaten beef for months after his first trip to one. Hodgins spotted a man heading his way. Luck was with him.

"Ya, I know who you're talking 'bout. Trouble makers, the lot of 'em." The burly man seemed to be in charge and, based on his hands, had worked hard all his life.

"The lot of them?" Hodgins asked. Were there more than two?"

"Four brothers, each one worse than the last."

"And you say their name is Clark? By any chance, does one of them have a mole?"

The burly man thought for a minute. "That'd be James. Looks like an hourglass, sitting on his ear lobe.

Most peculiar thing I ever did see."

"Do you have their address?"

"Check in the office. Probably got it there."

Hodgins got the address and went back to the station. The Clarks lived just outside the city. It was getting late, so he decided to head out in the morning, after talking to the coroner. He hadn't had time to find out if a full report was ready. Hodgins didn't even know what caliber of bullet killed Mr. Buckingham. Best to get that information before looking for the Clark brothers.

* * *

Hodgins took the streetcar to the station the next day, reading over all his notes along the way, before checking in with the coroner. The sun had burned off the morning chill, so he decided to walk the short distance from Station Four. The autopsy room was in the basement, with only two windows at street level. Stonehouse had both propped open.

"Airing out the room, Doctor?"

"Such a nice day, I thought it high time to circulate some fresh air. It's going to be quite ripe once summer hits. I assume this is not a social call? Looking for the report on the farmer?"

"Yes, have you completed your examination?"

"Have the report in my desk. Still have to write up a copy for you. Someone truly had it in for the old man. The bullet came first, likely killed him right off, or shortly after being shot. Bruising, but little bleeding around the puncture marks from the pitchfork. Same with the head wounds. If you recall, there wasn't much blood around the head when we found him. Mostly pooled around his upper body."

Dr. Stonehouse opened a drawer and pulled out several sheets of paper and handed them to Hodgins.

"Can you tell me what caliber the gun was?" Hodgins skimmed the pages, looking for the information.

"That's tricky, as you well know, but what you probably don't know is I'm somewhat of a gun expert. I find it fascinating how they work, and that a small bullet can cause so much damage. Based on the wound, I'm fairly confident saying it was made by a .22 caliber, most likely a Smith & Wesson. I'd guess a Model 1, but that's only because I'm partial to them. Common in the American Civil War."

Hodgins sighed. "So there's likely quite a few of them around now? Even up here?"

"Yes. Some Americans came up here after the war, and naturally they brought their firearms with them. A handy gun. Not too large, not too heavy. They made three different models of it. Extremely popular. Got interested in guns while travelling in Europe. Quite the gunsmiths over there. Superb craftsmanship."

"There's a lot I don't know about you, Stonehouse. I'd love to hear some of your stories, as would my wife. You'll have to join us for a meal one evening. Is there a Mrs. Stonehouse?"

"Never had time, what with schooling, work, and travel. Afraid it would take quite the woman to put up with my hours."

"Not much different from a copper's life. I myself managed to find the perfect wife, no, companion, confidant. Or maybe she found me. Still haven't figured that one out yet." Hodgins gave the report back and shook the doctor's hand.

"Thank you for the information. I'll be in touch about dinner."

Hodgins mumbled to himself as he made his way

back to the station. This new coroner was turning out to be quite an interesting chap. He hoped he could establish half the relationship he had with Dr. McKenzie. Wouldn't do to have a doctor that the police couldn't get along with. The coroner before McKenzie had been a miserable man, unwilling to part with any details before thoroughly completing his examination. At least McKenzie gave up information as he went, more than willing to speculate with Hodgins.

When he arrived at his desk, Hodgins flipped to the last of the comments in his notebook to the Clark's address. It hadn't occurred to him earlier that they were east of the Don River. Hodgins pulled out a map of the city to check the distance from their place to the Buckingham farm. The Clark's lived in the area people had begun to call Leslieville, on the east side of the railway line. The address was just north of Leslie and Son Nursery, on Audley. Hodgins decided to stop at the nursery and see if anyone there was acquainted with the brothers. Most people in that neighbourhood worked at the nursery at one time or another.

Hodgins walked down to John Mitchell's livery on

Duke Street and hired a buggy for the day. He guided the horse down to Queen Street and headed east towards the massive nursery on Kingston Road. The owner, George Leslie, wasn't available due to his duties as Postmaster for the Leslie Post Office, but the nursey manager had a few minutes free to speak with the detective.

"Yes, I know the Clarks. They all worked here, the father and the four sons. Lazy bunch, especially the father. And a drunk. The boys are just trouble-makers. Fired them months ago. My lad was in school with the second youngest, James. Always coming in late and disrupting class. Not many 'round here willing to hire them anymore. What've they done now?"

"Nothing, for certain. Just making inquiries. Problem on a farm they worked. Don't know if they were involved as they'd already been fired. Seems everyone has the same opinion of them. I would like to speak with them, though. Thank you for your time."

Hodgins lingered, enjoying the mixture of scents from the flowers. Much nicer than the cattle market. Not much grew outside yet, but there were many greenhouses here with all sorts of flowers in bloom.

The ride to the Clark home took only took six minutes. Their residence looked much the same as the rest on the street; single-story clapboard houses, inhabited by nursery or brick factory employees. Hodgins easily picked out the homes likely owned by gardeners.

When he found the Clark place, he took a moment to get a feel for the family. Weeds grew where grass should have been. A broken chair sat near the front door on a porch that had seen better days. It clearly hadn't been painted since the day it was built. Hodgins took a deep breath and approached the porch.

The step groaned under his weight, but held. He manoeuvred around the nails poking through, both on the stairs and floor-boards of the porch. The front door opened as he reached to knock.

CHAPTER NINE

"Whadda ya want?" The man who opened the door appeared to be a little older than Hodgins, but twice the weight. The man wasn't fat, though. He had the muscles of someone used to doing heavy work. Hodgins definitely didn't wish to get into a fist fight with this one.

"Are you Mr. Clark?"

"I ain't done nothing wrong, copper." He started to close the door.

"I'm looking for your sons, James and Peter."

Clark stopped, door half shut. "What ya want with my boys?"

"Just to talk to them. They were employed at the Buckingham farm recently and I need to ask them a few questions."

"Well, they ain't here. Gone to Elora to work in the flour mill. My brother-in-law works there. Fraser's. Ya wanna talk to 'em, go to Elora." Clark slammed the door shut.

Hodgins stared at the peeling paint. "Thank you for your time, Mr. Clark." He went back to the buggy and headed to the station.

* * *

By the time he arrived back it started to rain. Hodgins shook off his coat and hat before hanging them on the hook by the pot-belly stove. When he turned around, he almost collided with Riddell.

"Looks like you could use this." He held out a large mug of steaming tea.

"You're a saint, Riddell. Come into my office." Hodgins wrapped both hands around the mug and took a few sips before moving.

"Those Clark boys are suspicious. Seems they've taken off to Elora. Could be a coincidence they've moved right after the murder, but everyone I've spoken to had nothing good to say about them. The entire family actually." He put the tea on his desk and sat. Notes about the murder still lay scattered across the desk. Hodgins tossed his notebook on top of the papers.

"So far they're my only suspects. Have you turned up anything on the family?"

"Nothing new about the son. Went through the files dating back to 1840s and found a few old reports about minor fights Charlie instigated. All several years old. I'm still searching. Oh, Harrington fell at home and sprained his ankle. Doctor told him to stay off it a few days."

"Once Harrington's back, send him to check the land records. He can do that sitting down. What about the brother-in-law? Did you find out anything? Why they moved?"

"Yes, I spoke to some of the businesses around his old store. Sounds like he was simply too busy. Image that. Moving because you're successful."

"Some people prefer a quieter, easy life. He moved to a small town that's growing. Probably made enough to be comfortable and should have enough customers to keep food on the table. When I spoke with him, he seemed quite content. Keep asking around, though."

Hodgins searched through the papers on his desk. "Where's that blasted train schedule for the Grey and Bruce?" He pulled open the drawers and found it

sitting on the top of another pile of papers. "Finally."
He sat it on the desktop and spread it out, careful not
to rip the schedule.

Riddell watched as Hodgins ran his index finger
down the columns, searching for the stop at Union
Station. "When will you be leaving, sir?"

"Looks like there's a train at eight, Monday. Why
can't they schedule these things to leave at a
respectable hour? And it doesn't even go where I
need." He rummaged through his desk for more
schedules. "Three trains! It'll take all day to get there.
It is what it is, I suppose. Maybe one day they'll figure
out a way to make them run faster and more often with
less transfers."

"That would be nice," Riddell agreed.

"Can't understand why people won't speak with us.
It's almost as though they don't want the criminals
caught. With any luck I'll be bringing the culprit back
with me."

Riddell hesitated before commenting. "If these
Clark chaps are as bad as everyone says, are you sure
you should be going alone? I could go with you."

Hodgins looks up, surprised at Riddell's

suggestion. "You? That's not a bad idea. It's going to be a long train ride and I wouldn't mind the company. I seem to always take Barnes with me. No reason not to take you or one of the other lads sometimes. Can't be playing favourites. Meet me at Union station a little before eight, Monday morning, and pack your rucksack. Won't be able to make a round trip in one day."

Riddell headed to the file room. Hodgins gulped down the last of his tea before donning his wet overcoat and heading home to break the news to Cordelia. While walking, Hodgins tried to imagine Delia's reaction when he said he'd be out of town again. Normally, she wouldn't be fussed, but she'd been tired lately running around after the twins. Sara could only help so much – her chores and school work came first. By the time he walked through the front door he had formulated a solution.

* * *

Hodgins sat in the front room with his family, watching their eldest daughter and the dog, Scraps, play with the twins. Six months ago, if someone had suggested he'd become a father again, he would have sent them to the insane asylum. But when he arrested a woman with twins, he just couldn't let the babies go into care. He'd seen the inside of the local orphanage more than once during his career as an office. The headmaster tried his best, but there were too many children to care for, the older ones getting into trouble daily. Hodgins had the means to provide for the twins, and he and Cordelia had hoped for more children, so when Sara suggested adoption, they'd agreed.

"Sorry, Delia, but it can't be helped. There's a vicious killer, or killers on the loose and I need to find them. My best guess is one or both of the Clark boys, and guess is all it is. Much as I hate to admit it, I have nothing to go on."

"I know, Bertie, and I do understand. I'm just tired. I'd forgotten how much work babies can be, especially when they start walking." She thought for a moment. "If you think you'll be gone for a day or two, maybe I'll ask Mother to stay with me."

Hodgins pulled his wife close. "My job keeps pulling me away, so, as much as I'd like to help you more, I can't. I came up with an idea on my way home tonight. When this is over, why don't we see about hiring some help? Just until the twins are in school. We can afford it. Someone to come in for a few hours a day?"

Cordelia squeezed Hodgins tight. "That would be a God-send. I'll make inquires. Mother may know someone." She pulled back. "Mother! She'll be so upset if we don't ask her."

"Don't take this the wrong way, but I can't have her in this house every day. I love your parents as though they were my own, but after ten years of living in their house, I can't have her constantly in mine. You know she disapproves of my work and takes every opportunity to let me know you could have done much better than marry a lowly police officer."

"I know. She loves you, in her own way." Cordelia laughed. "Don't look at me like that. She does care for you. All she wants is for me to be happy, and I am. Deliriously happy. I don't believe she'll want the job anyway. I'll make sure she knows just how much work twins are and how tired she'll be. It really is a job for a younger woman. Someone like Violet would be perfect, except she'll likely be married to Henry soon and will be spending all her time setting up house and getting used to married life. Didn't you say Barnes is supposed to talk to Violet's father before Bridget's engagement party tonight?"

"Why don't you speak with Violet? Maybe she has a friend who wouldn't mind working for a lowly police officer."

Cordelia gave Hodgins a light tap on the arm and smiled. "Are you making fun of my mother?"

"At every opportunity. Now, I think it's high time we put in an appearance at the party next door. I suppose we need to take a gift?"

"That's all in hand. Remember that lace tablecloth I crocheted? It doesn't fit our table, so I thought I'd give it to them as a wedding gift, and the matching antimacassars as an engagement gift."

Hodgins kissed Delia on the cheek. "Beautiful, practical, and smart. How did I get so lucky?"

* * *

When they arrived at the party, Delia placed their gift on the table and Hodgins went in search of Barnes. He spotted him in a room on the opposite side of the hall with Violet's father. Hodgins pretended to examine a painting hanging beside the door. Barnes and Mr.

Halloway stood by the fireplace, just out of earshot. Hodgins watched as Barnes fidgeted.

Halloway became impatient and bellowed. "Out with it, lad. I need to attend to my sister."

Hodgins grinned, remembering a similar discussion with Cordelia's father. He watched as Barnes straightened up and took a deep breath.

"Bertie. Whatever are you doing? Come, join the party."

Cordelia placed her arm around Hodgins waist and tugged him across the hall to the engagement party.

"Delia, your timing couldn't be worse. Barnes was just about to ask for Violet's hand."

"Shame on you for eavesdropping. You'll find out soon enough. You know Henry won't be able to keep quiet about it."

Violet had Barnes' attention the rest of the evening. Hodgins tried to read the expression on his face and couldn't decide if the lad looked dejected from being told he couldn't marry Violet, or terrified at the prospect of having to propose.

* * *

Sunday morning, Delia dressed the twins in the little

outfits she'd made and put ribbons in their fine, strawberry-blond hair. "If people didn't know better, they'd assume the twins were mine. Just enough red, but not too much." She smoothed their dresses and admired her handiwork. "Beautiful."

"If Barnes plucked up the courage this morning as planned, there should be a wedding announcement at the service. The church will be buzzing with people congratulating the couple and fussing over the twins. Everyone ready to go?"

They joined everyone on the walk to the Primitive Methodist Church. The neighbours fussed over the toddlers, who enjoyed all the new attention.

Hodgins nudged Cordelia. "There's Barnes up ahead. Guess it's now or never."

They watched as the young couple fell behind her parents, allowing Barnes a bit of privacy.

When Violet squealed and threw her arms around Barnes, Sara clapped. "Oh, another wedding." The twins clapped with her.

* * *

After the service, the minister invited Henry and Violet to stand with him on the church steps so everyone could congratulate them.

The Hodgins family stood on the sidewalk to allow the congregation the opportunity to meet Holly and Ivy. A few made snide remarks, but the twins were too young to understand.

"We'll have to arrange a baptism soon." Delia picked up Ivy. "I'll speak with the reverend another day. These two are worn out. Time to head home."

Hodgins picked up Holly, nodding at Barnes before following Delia home.

* * *

Hodgins rose early the next day and took Scraps for a walk. He enjoyed the quiet of the morning. It helped organize his thoughts. Now that Delia was preoccupied with the new babies, he had trouble finding time to speak with her about his latest case. She had a way of looking at things that left him amazed. Often, one little thing that he couldn't figure would be so clear to her. Maybe talking to the dog would help.

"What do you think, boy? Are the Clark's killers, or just bullies? Maybe bullies gone too far?"

Scraps cocked his head.

"What about Buckingham's son? He's not the

nicest person, and didn't seem all that upset about his father's death. The farm will likely go to him. Could be a provision in his will for his wife to have control until her death. Remind me to check that, will you?"

Scraps woofed softly.

"Good boy. It think it's time to head back or I'll miss my train."

CHAPTER TEN

Riddell made it to the train station before Hodgins, and sat waiting on one of the wooden benches along-side the booth. He stood when Hodgins approached. "Already bought our tickets, Detective."

"Thank you, Riddell. Nice to see you're on top of things, and prompt too. You've been on the force longer than Barnes. Why haven't you expressed interest in becoming a detective before?"

"Well, to be honest, I was afraid to approach you."

"That bad, was I?" Hodgins laughed. "Yes, I suppose I was a little unapproachable. Do my job, go home to my family. Didn't really bother much with the lads. Was I too terrible?"

"No, sir. You were never unkind to anyone, and always fair. You just kept to yourself. Seeing you take time to teach Henry made me unafraid to speak up the other day."

"Glad to hear it. So, what have you learned about this case? Do you have any ideas? I'll admit I'm at a loss."

"I think Charlie did it."

"Buckingham's son? What makes you say that? Barnes did mention you had strong feelings around him."

"I knew him in school. We weren't in the same class, but he's the same age as my eldest brother, Will. Charlie broke Will's nose once, just for fun. I wouldn't put it past him to do something to his father. They never got along all that well. I've continued digging through the old files, looking for reports on all the incidents I could remember. Even asked Will and he told me of other things that were never reported."

Hodgins nodded. "Bit of a stretch to go from being a schoolyard bully to murdering your father, but he is on the list. We just have no solid evidence. Hell, we have no shaky evidence."

The train pulled in, drowning out Hodgins' voice. Between the shrill whistle, the hiss of steam, and the squealing of the breaks, it was impossible to have a conversation.

"What was that, sir?"

"I said, we have no evidence. Let's find a spot and we'll continue this on the train."

They settled into the seats in the back corner of the passenger car and Hodgins rested his notebook on his lap. "Right now we need to concentrate on those Clark brothers. I believe one of them was in town shortly before we were alerted to Buckingham's murder. Waved a gun around. Scared one woman so bad she fainted. And now they've conveniently left town."

"That is suspicious. They were fired, weren't they? I suppose people have murdered for less reasons. Henry, Constable Barnes, said they've gone to work with an uncle."

"Yes, and it's all right to call him Henry. No need to be formal."

The whistle blew again, and the train jolted forward. Hodgins' notebook fell on the floor. Riddell leaned down and retrieved it.

"Thank you, Riddell. It's Thomas, isn't it?"

"Yes, but most everyone just calls me Tom."

"Do you or your brother know any of the Clarks?

"Afraid not. We live in a different part of town.

When we get back, I'll check around Leslieville. See if I can find some of their school mates and neighbours. Maybe they have more information." Riddell made notes in his book as he yawned.

Hodgins yawned in return. "It's a long ride. Let's see if we can get a bit of sleep on this rickety old Pullman."

* * *

The train pulled into Orangeville before noon, but their connection didn't leave until 5:00 p.m. Unfortunately, the next leg of the journey only took them as far as Cataract Junction. At least that wait wasn't as long. Both men were exhausted when they finally arrived in Elora.

Hodgins glanced at the clock hanging from the platform roof. Almost 8:00 p.m. He flagged a buggy waiting nearby. As they rode into town, they passed several farms. The roar of the gorge made it impossible for conversation. He instructed the driver to take them straight to Fraser's flour mill. A light flickered inside, but most workers had gone home for the day.

Hodgins approached the first person he saw. "Looking for Mr. Clark."

"Around the side, by the wheel."

Hodgins and Riddell made their way along the narrow path leading to the thirty-foot water wheel. It wasn't turning. A middle-aged man balanced on one of the cross-bars.

"Are you Mr. Clark?" Hodgins yelled.

"Busy. Come back later."

"Toronto Constabulary. We need a word."

"You'll have to wait. Need to get this thing fixed." Clark continued to climb the wheel.

"What now?" Riddell asked.

"We wait. Let's go inside and see if either of his nephews are here."

The remaining men were on their way home. When Hodgins asked if James or Peter Clark worked there, all they got in reply were shrugs and head shakes. The third person was slightly more helpful.

"Don't know their names, but two lads started just the other day. Heard they were related to the boss. Haven't seen them today, though." He took off his flat cap and smacked it against his leg, sending a cloud of white flour dust everywhere, including on Hodgins and Riddell.

Riddell started coughing so Hodgins sent him outside, then turned back to the employee.

"What's wrong with the wheel?'"

"Don't rightly know. It ground to a stop 'bout a couple of hours ago. Mr. Clark's been trying to fix it. Might take quite some time. Knowing him, he'll be out there 'till midnight trying to get it going. Can't do much if we don't got a working wheel. Almost done bagging up what flour we managed to get this morning. Sorry 'bout your suit."

"Never mind about that. Do you know where Mr. Clark lives?"

"Why sure. Big house on the corner of Mill and Kertland. Just a few blocks over. Can't miss it."

"Thank you." Hodgins joined Riddell outside, who was trying to wipe the white power off his trousers.

"Need a proper brush for that. Hand won't do much. The Clark brothers aren't here. Might be at their uncle's. Why don't we try there, then find someplace to grab a bite and lodgings? Looks like we'll be spending at least one night here. Not going to get much out of Clark until he fixes that wheel."

It didn't take long for them to find Clark's home.

"The employee at the flour mill wasn't kidding when he said we couldn't miss it." Hodgins stood in front of the wrought iron gate in the fence surrounding the largest house on the block. "Must be doing well at the mill."

The gate opened with a small creak, and Hodgins and Riddell strolled up to the front door. A slip of a woman, maybe in her fifties, opened the door.

"Can I help you?" The scent of a roast cooking wafted out the door. Riddell's stomach growled.

The constable's face turned pink. "Apologies, ma'am."

Hodgins forced himself not to grin. "Is this the Clark residence?"

She nodded.

"I'm Detective Hodgins, from the Toronto Constabulary. We're looking for Mr. Clark's nephews, Peter and James. Are they here?"

"What have they done now? Come in, please."

She showed them to a large sitting room to the left of the front door. A low fire smoldered in the ornate brick fireplace. She nattered as they walked.

"Known those boys since they were just sprigs.

Always getting into trouble. Maybe if their father hadn't moved them to the city they would've settled down by now."

She ushered them to a pair of large chairs by the fire. "Been damp lately. Colder here as we're so close to the river. I see you've been to the mill. Wait right here."

She scurried out and returned in less than a minute with a horse-hair brush. "This should take that flour out of your clothes. Don't worry about making a mess. Every evening this place is full of flour dust. I don't bother cleaning up any more until everyone's gone to bed. Now, you were asking about the boys."

"Yes, we'd like to speak with them. A former employer of theirs was found murdered and we need to confirm their whereabouts." Hodgins took out his notebook and flipped to a clean page. "I didn't get your name, ma'am."

"It's Mrs. Campbell. Peter's around here somewhere, but I don't know where James went. They said Mr. Clark sent them home when the wheel broke. Been doing that a lot lately. He'll have to replace it soon, but that means shutting down. I'll find Peter and send him in."

She left them alone, and Hodgins took the opportunity to brush off the flour. He moved away from the rug to stand on the hardwood floor by the window. "Easier to sweep up on the floor. No point giving the poor women more work than necessary." Hodgins brushed his trousers, removed his jacket and did the same. He went back to the fireplace and handed the brush over to Riddell.

By the time Riddell had removed as much powder as he could from his uniform, a rough looking lad entered the room. "Housekeeper said you were looking for me. Said someone's died."

Riddell corrected him. "Murdered actually. Are you Peter Clark?"

Peter saunter over to a settee and sat, flinging one leg over the arm. "Ya. I'm Peter. So, who's counting worms?"

Riddell started to say something about the young man's disrespectful comment, but Hodgins stopped him.

"Leave it." He turned back to Peter. "Mr. Buckingham was murdered recently, and we understand you and your brother worked for him for a short time. Can you tell me why you left his employ?"

"Left his employ? That's a good one. The old codger fired us. Me and James could lift twice as much as old Smitty, but that weren't good enough."

Hodgins indicated for Riddell to take notes. "So you didn't leave on good terms?"

"Oh, sure. We're the best of friends." Peter laughed so hard he almost fell off the settee.

Hodgins waited until the young man composed himself. "Where were you and your brother on May 3?"

"Hmm, right here I reckon."

"Are you certain? We have witnesses that saw you both in Toronto the day before, firing a gun on Wellington Street, by Prescott Brewing."

Peter yawned. "Really? Never was one for bothering to keep track of the days. All I can tell you for certain is we took the train 'bout a week ago. Maybe Mrs. Campbell or Uncle Sam can tell you when. Is that all you wanted? I'm meeting friends soon."

Hodgins grew impatient with the reckless young man and tapped his pencil on his closed notebook, keeping time with the mantle clock over the fireplace. "A man has been murdered and all you can think about is going out? Do you realize both you and your brother are suspects?"

Peter sat up. "Suspects? Me and James? What jolly fun. How are you going to prove it? We haven't been out to the farm since we were fired. And being in town doesn't mean anything. Lots of people are in town with guns." He stood and headed to the door. "I'll let James know. He'll get a hoot out of it, I'm sure."

They heard Peter laugh as he headed upstairs.

Riddell stood by the fireplace. "Well, of all the nerve. Who does he think he is?"

"He thinks he's a brash young man and out of our reach. And he's right. We have nothing to connect him or his brother to the murder. He seems to have forgotten they went back to see if Buckingham would re-hire them. I wonder what else he's conveniently forgotten to mention. Hopefully the housekeeper can remember when they arrived." Hodgins walked into the hallway and called for her.

Mrs. Campbell came out of the kitchen, wiping her hands on her apron. "Yes? Is there something else?"

"Just one question and we'll be on our way. Do you remember when the Clarks arrived? What day it was?"

"Let me think. It was the day after the telegram arrived." She scurried to a small table just inside the front door and opened the single drawer. "Here is it. May 2. Says they'll be arriving on the train the next day, and they did. Mr. Clark went to pick up his nephews from the eight o'clock train, but it was almost an hour late."

"Thank you, Mrs. Campbell. We'll be on our way."

Hodgins and Riddell headed back to the main street and found the local tavern. "After we've eaten, we can head over to the mill and see if Mr. Clark is ready to speak with us, then we need to find lodgings. Damn complicated ride, what with having to change trains so much."

They ordered their meal and were told they could find lodgings at Allen's boarding house. Once their bellies were full, and accommodation arranged, they made their way back to the mill. It was dark but Mr. Clark was still there, standing by the stationary wheel, cursing.

"Mr. Clark. We're investigating a murder and it's

very important that we speak with you."

He threw down a rag, covered with grease, his hands still dirty. "May as well get it over with. Ain't going to get that thing working tonight. Have to get new parts made up. This is going to set me back days, and I don't even want to think about the cost. Mr. Fraser won't be happy. Let's go into my office. Not overly comfortable, but it's better than standing out here watching our profits wash down the Grand River."

Hodgins watched the water flow before he followed Clark inside. "Quite the impressive river. We've got nothing quite so splendid in Toronto."

Clark grunted. "It's impressive when the wheel is working. Several mills along the banks here depend on the river."

As they entered, Clark picked up some rags by the door and continued wiping the grease off his hands. "Office is this way."

A single door sat at the far end of the building. The office was small, but at least it was reasonably free of the flour dust.

Clark dropped onto the chair behind a small desk,

and sighed. "Exhausting work, trying to fix a wheel. Getting too old to climb up and down. Don't have any children of my own, so when my brother sent that telegram I hoped one of the boys would eventually be able to take over. So far, they haven't been much help. What is it that requires a visit from the Toronto Constabulary? You mentioned a murder."

Hodgins spent a few minutes rehashing what he'd told the housekeeper about the murder. "We've interviewed Peter, but James wasn't about. Can you confirm they arrived May 3?"

"Yes, that sounds right. I picked them up myself the day after the telegram arrived. Those boys have always been easily bored and seem to enjoy causing hardships to others. But murder? Honestly? I can imagine them going too far and someone getting seriously injured, possibly even accidently killed. But they're both too lazy to plan a murder. Maybe if my brother hadn't moved, or the boys came out when they were younger, I could've turned them around. It would take a miracle to fix them now. Still have hope for the youngest, if I can convince my brother to send him over."

"Thank you for your candour, Mr. Clark. I think that's all for now. I'll be in touch if I have any further questions."

The shops they passed on the way to Allen's Boarding House had long since closed. They stopped in front of the general store and Hodgins admired a piece of jewellery Cordelia would like. Unfortunately, they'd been leaving before the store opened in the morning. They made their way along the deserted streets to the boarding house.

"Train leaves before eight tomorrow morning, so we should get some sleep," Hodgins said. The rooms were small, but Hodgins didn't mind as they were clean and comfortable.

* * *

Hodgins woke shortly after six. He let Riddell have another half hour before knocking on his door. They'd arranged an early breakfast, and Mrs. Allen even packed food for their long train ride home. The train left on schedule and, just over an hour later, they transferred at Cataract Junction to wait over an hour and half for the next train. They arrived in Orangeville just as the Toronto engine pulled out of the station.

"Run," Hodgins called to Riddell. The detective grabbed his rucksack and hopped off the train before it came to a complete stop. Riddell hesitated, but followed. The conductor yelled, but the hiss from the steam made it impossible to hear his curses.

Hodgins ran down the platform and threw his bag onto the back of the train, then grabbed the rail on the stairs of the caboose, hauling himself up. He turned back.

"Hurry, Riddell. Toss me your bag." Hodgins caught it and placed it beside his.

Riddell ran along-side but couldn't quite reach. Hodgins held onto the rail and leaned out. Their fingers touched. "Faster."

Riddell took larger strides. Hodgins strained and grabbed the constable's hand to pull him on the train.

CHAPTER ELEVEN

It was late afternoon by the time they arrived back at Station Four, completely exhausted, sweaty, and more than a little dusty.

"I've never run so much in my life." Hodgins flopped onto the nearest chair.

Riddell perched on the closest desk. "I was on the track team and thought I was still in shape. My legs haven't ached so much in years."

"Sitting on the train for such a long period hasn't helped. Every muscle in my body is stiff. I think a good long soak is in order."

Barnes appeared with two steaming cups of tea, interrupting their griping. "Here you go, sir. And one for you, Tom. You look like you walked back from Elora."

Hodgins blew on his tea before taking a sip. "Pure heaven. The tea on the train tasted like someone's bath water. Take note, Riddell. Best way to move up the ranks is being able anticipate your superior's every need."

"Did you find the Clark brothers?" Barnes asked.

"Yes. Well, one of them. They're both there, but James wasn't around. If he's anything like his brother, they're a lazy, disrespectful lot. Even their uncle didn't have a good word to say. They have no regard for anyone, and don't seem to take well to work." Hodgins took another sip of tea."

"I'm confident they didn't do it, as they were on the train at the time, but we need to make further inquiries. My instincts tell me it wasn't Smitty, even though he can't tell us anything. Unless one of you knows a good medium."

Riddell put his tea cup down and crossed his arms. "I still think it was Charlie. He's got a history of violence, and stands to inherit."

Hodgins nodded. "Could be, but you are rather biased." Hodgins held up a hand when Riddell started to reply. "We won't stop looking into him, but we can't focus solely on Charlie."

Barnes rushed to his desk and returned with his

notebook. "I looked into their neighbour, Mr. Logan." He flipped through the pages. "Here it is. Only two months ago they had an argument over land boundaries. Went to court. Logan said it ended amicably, but if it went that far, there must be bad feelings."

Hodgins reached for the notebook and read Barnes' comments. "I do recall he mentioned something about one of the fields, but didn't elaborate." He returned the notebook to Barnes. "Did you see the court records?"

"No, it was too late in the day. One of the clerks is going to pull the record books for me tomorrow. Harrington said he'll be able to assist, so maybe he can pick them up, and search the land records while he's there."

"Good idea." Hodgins turned to Riddell. "You may as well continue searching for more records on the son. I have a feeling you will anyway."

"Yes, sir. Right away." Riddell stood, but fell back against the desk. "Leg's still a little stiff."

"Go home. It can wait until tomorrow. I think we both need a good bath and some home cooking. Don't worry about coming in on time. I plan on sleeping in. Need to be fresh when we continue digging."

Riddell's eyebrows shot up in surprise. "Come in late? Won't the inspector mind?"

"If he asks, I'll tell him you and Detective Hodgins are following up on a lead," Barnes said.

Hodgins slapped Riddell on the back. "It's settled then. We'll sleep in and arrive back here fully refreshed by, what? Ten?"

"Ten it is, sir. Hopefully my legs cooperate."

* * *

Hodgins sent Sara off to mind the twins while he helped his wife clean up and wash the dishes. "I'm at loss to figure this one out, Delia. There's nothing to go on. No witnesses, no clues of any sort. I don't know how we're going to figure out who murdered Mr. Buckingham unless someone confesses."

"You'll figure it out. There has to be something. You just haven't found it yet. Didn't you say you were certain their neighbour was hiding something?"

Hodgins nodded. "Barnes discovered there was a disagreement about land boundaries. I've got the lads looking in the land and court records. Maybe something will turn up soon."

They jumped at the sound of breaking glass.

"Mamma!" Sara shrieked.

CHAPTER TWELVE

Scraps barked and the toddlers wailed. Both Hodgins and Delia ran into the front room. A vase lay in pieces just inside the doorway. Sara cuddled the twins while the dog ran in circles.

Hodgins winced as he knelt to clean up the mess while Delia checked the twins. The muscles in his legs were stiffer than ever.

"What happened?" She wiped a spot of blood off Ivy's arm. "Just a tiny scratch. Nothing to be concerned about."

Sara sniffled. "Ivy was trying to run. She grabbed the table and fell. The table came down, but didn't hit her. It happened so fast."

Delia put her arm around Sara's shoulder while cradling Ivy in her other arm. "Don't fret, dear. Why, when you were about Ivy's age you broke my mother's favourite plate. When babies turn into toddlers these things are to be expected. Ivy's fine. We'll just have to rearrange all the breakables."

She kissed Sara on the forehead, gathered up the twins and took them upstairs, Sara close behind. Hodgins disposed of the broken porcelain, mopped up the spilled water, and found another vase for the flowers before settling down to read the newspaper while the water boiled for his soak in the tin bathtub in the corner of the kitchen.

* * *

The next morning Hodgins strolled into Station House Four a few minutes before ten. He spotted Riddell coming out of the back with a cup of tea.

"Couldn't wait, I see. Did you find out anything new? Afraid I'm at a loss."

Riddell frowned. "Same here, sir. Just having a spot of tea to clear my throat before I go back to the files. My mouth is rather dry from the dust on them."

"Keep digging. Someone has to have a reason for wanting Buckingham dead." Hodgins went into his office and reviewed his notes.

Twenty minutes later, the desk sergeant knocked on his door. "Sorry to interrupt, sir, but there's a boy asking to speak with you. About the Buckingham murder."

Hodgins put his notes aside. "Send him in."

A minute later the sergeant was back. "This is Mr. Clark." He closed the door and returned to his post.

Hodgins rose and shook the young man's hand. "Mr. Clark? Any relation to Peter and James?"

"Yes, sir. Them's my older brothers."

Hodgins opened his notebook. "Have a seat. And what brings you here?"

Clark perched on the edge of the chair and fiddled with a button on his shirt. "Well, it's been weighin' mighty heavy on my mind."

"Take your time. Whatever it is, you'll feel better once you tell me. Would you like some tea?"

"No, ta." He stood to leave. "I can't. Pa will kill me."

Hodgins hoped the lad had information that could break the case. He couldn't let him leave so soon. "Wait. If you know something about Mr. Buckingham's murder, it's your obligation to tell me."

Clark stopped, hand on the door handle. "I don't know."

"Please. Sit down. Take your time." Hodgins joined Clark at the door. "You've come all the way here. Why not get it off your chest?"

Clark let go of the handle and turned. "Well …"

Hodgins took the boy's arm and gently guided him back to the chair. The detective noticed this one wasn't as rough and disrespectful as Peter. Maybe the uncle was right about having hope for him.

As soon as Clark sat, he started talking – too fast for Hodgins to keep up.

"Slow down, son. Take a deep breath and start again, slower this time."

"It's my brother, James. I think he done it. Kilt that farmer."

Hodgins picked up his pencil. "What makes you say that? Did he say as much?"

"No. Heard him and Peter talking afore they went to Uncle Sam's. They thought I was sleeping. We share a room." Clark sniffled and ran his hand under his nose. "Said no one'd catch 'em out in Elora."

"Did Peter actually say he killed Mr. Buckingham?"

"I peeked out from under the covers. He had a gun. I can't say nothin' more." Clark bolted for the door and ran out.

"Blast." Hodgins ran out after him, but by the time he reached the front, the boy was nowhere in sight.

Barnes joined Hodgins at the station door. "Who was that?"

"Another Clark brother. Didn't get his first name. Said he heard his brothers talking and thinks they killed Buckingham. Mentioned a gun then ran out."

"Must have been hard coming here to tattle on his brothers. If what you told me about his family is true, he must be terrified what they'll do to him if they find out."

Hodgins closed the door. His thoughts went back to Christmas. His brother had been the main suspect in not one, but two murders and every piece of evidence lead back to him. "I know how the lad feels. Come into my office. See if we can't figure something out."

Barnes ran to his own desk and grabbed his notebook before joining Hodgins. He turned to his notes and sat in the chair in front of the desk. "This one is a real puzzler, sir."

The detective pulled out a piece of foolscap. "Let's

list everyone involved and see if we can positively eliminate anyone. May as well start with the family." He listed the names down the left side.

Lenore Buckingham – victim's wife

Charlie Buckingham – son

Mrs. Adelia Buckingham – son's wife

Mrs. Beatrice McTaggart – daughter

Mr. Joseph McTaggart – daughter's husband

Mr. Daniel Logan – neighbour

Peter & James Clark – fired

Hodgins tapped his pencil on the page. "We know the Clark's were in Elora at the time. I think we can also eliminate the daughter and her husband. They were miles away. I suppose the wife could have done it, but she was so upset, I can't imagine she's guilty. She does have the strength and was alone at the time, though. The question is, was she upset because her husband was killed, or because she did it? Maybe it was accident? I'll leave her on the list, but I doubt she's guilty. That leaves her son, his wife, and Mr. Logan. Don't think young Mrs. Buckingham could even kill a bug. But that son – I just don't like or trust him. And Logan seemed to think it necessary to hide that land dispute from us."

"I agree about the son." Barnes twirled his pencil. "He's not at all likeable, and does have a history of violence. I wonder if Riddell has found anything other than schoolyard brawls? I disagree that we can eliminate the daughter and her husband. They could have hired someone."

Hodgins thought about his new twins and their natural mother. She'd hired someone to murder her husband, and framed Hodgins' brother in the process. "Yes, that's a possibility. And we can't eliminate the neighbour, Mr. Logan. Too bad the hired hand, Smitty, died. I think we can eliminate him, but unless we find the real killer, we'll never know for certain."

Barnes scanned his notes from their earlier trip to Collingwood. "Mr. Smith's daughter mentioned he killed her mother. I know nothing was proven, but there must have been some history of violent behaviour for her to believe her father capable of killing her mother. And she truly does hate him. Not at all concerned that he'd drowned."

Hodgins dropped the pencil on his desk and leaned back in his chair, hands clasped behind his head. "Well, that is a head scratcher. No foul play involved. The local authorities put it down to a boating accident. But did he take the boat out with the intention of dying or was it just plain stupidity? He may have murdered his wife all those years ago in a fit of anger. Same thing may have happened on the farm, and he went back to his roots to sentence himself for both acts."

"From the description we've been given of him, I don't think he would have been strong enough to drive a pitchfork though Mr. Buckingham's chest. Mrs. Buckingham mentioned Smitty was strong, but they felt the need to hire the Clark brothers, so he can't be all that strong. He was an old man after all." Barnes closed his notebook and placed it on the edge of the desk. "Is there someone else we don't know about?"

"I can't think of anyone else, and I agree. Smitty probably didn't do it. As you said, he was elderly and the Buckinghams did think it necessary to hire extra help. Have you found anything that would give either of their children a motive? Do we know about the disposition of his property and belongings? And is there anything more on the disagreement with Logan?"

"Still checking on all that. I stopped in to see how

Harrington's doing. He said he can return to work tomorrow for a short while. I told him to go to the land office. Hope I didn't overstep, sir."

Hodgins leaned farther back in his chair, the front legs lifted off the floor. "Not at all. We already discussed having him do that as it's easily done on his arse." The chair banged on the floor when he leaned forward. "Glad to hear he's up to returning. Might be a while before he's able to go back out on the beat again."

Hodgins looked up and saw Riddell coming out of the file room. He called him in. "Did you find anything?"

Riddell waved a file. "Right here. A complaint was lodged against Charlie just last year. Rather strange. Seems he assaulted a man right in front of the Bank of British North America on the corner of Yonge and Wellington Streets. Next day, the man withdrew his complaint. Think I should go and see if anyone at the bank remembers. Maybe even have a chat with …" he looked in the file. "Mr. Austin. The man he allegedly struck. His address is right here."

"Good idea. Track down Austin. Barnes, see if you

can find out if the son gets the farm. Talk to the Buckingham's again. If he left a will, get a copy. I'm going to see if I can find out what the kerfuffle was between Buckingham and Logan. If there was a dispute over the property, there has to be something in the court records. I'd also like to have a look at the McTaggart's finances." Hodgins stepped out from behind his desk, and waved his hands at the two constables. "Off with you now. I'll be expecting a full report in the morning."

CHAPTER THIRTEEN

Next morning, Hodgins arrived at the station to find Barnes waiting for him. "Sir, I'm glad you're still here. Good thing I went back out to the Buckingham's. Seems one item is missing. When Mr. Buckingham's belongings were returned to the widow his pocket watch wasn't included. It was a special watch, meant to go to their son. Handed down for the past three generations. Mrs. Buckingham is quite upset. Gold watch, on a chain, inscription inside that says, *With hard work and dedication, anything is possible*. I'll check around the pawn shops and see if anyone's tried to hock it. Worth a pretty penny, I'm sure."

Hodgins slapped him on the back. "Don't tell me we've finally caught a break? With any luck, whoever took it tries to sell or pawn it. Maybe we can get a description and match him to one of our suspects. Might have to lean on the brokers to get them to talk.

You up for that, Henry?"

"Yes, sir. I can handle myself. Someone's killed a defenseless old man and I intend to do whatever necessary to make sure he pays for it."

Barnes walked back to his desk, head held high, determined to find the watch. Ten minutes later, he knocked on the detectives' door.

"Sir? I've been thinking." The constable paced around the office, wringing his hands.

"Sit down, Henry. You're making me dizzy."

Barnes sat, but immediately popped up again. "I'm sorry, sir, but I don't believe I can talk to the pawn brokers myself. They're a tough lot, and look at me. I couldn't even scare a fly. They'll laugh me out of their shops."

Hodgins agreed with him, but didn't want to come out and say so. "Would you prefer it if I found someone else go in your stead?"

"Heavens no." Barnes seemed even more distressed. "What would the lads think of me if I can't do my job? But if I went with you …"

"Then you'd be assisting me. Nothing unusual about that, is there?"

Barnes mood brightened. "That would be grand." His smile disappeared. "You don't think me chicken, do you?"

"No, not at all. You've been a constable barely a year. It takes time to learn how to handle some of the rougher people in the city." Hodgins thought for a moment. "Have you joined the YMCA yet? They can teach you to box, and build up your muscles. Didn't my brother offer to help train you?"

Barnes shrugged. "Haven't gotten around to it."

"There's a lot you've been putting off lately. At least you finally proposed. "

"Yes, but I still have to get a ring."

Hodgins got up and stood beside Barnes. "And Delia is already helping arrange an engagement party for you."

Barnes grinned and nodded.

"That's a start. Now back to business, lad. Do you have a list of pawn brokers? I know some of them, but they seem to move frequently."

Barnes removed a loose sheet of paper from his notebook. "Right here."

"Come on then. May as well get started. Who's first

on the list?"

Barnes unfolded the page and read it. "There are three on Queen Street. May as well start there."

Hodgins hailed a cab as it had started to rain and he forgot his umbrella. Fortunately, the horse didn't mind getting wet. The ride down was quick and they got off at the entrance to Victoria Lane, a few blocks east of Yonge Street. He'd been to various pawnbrokers over the years and had become used to most of them being hidden down the side streets.

Unfortunately, Barnes was a little jumpy. "I'm glad it's not nighttime. Can't see there being much light down here." He stood at the entrance to the walkway, taking in the area. "Imagine, setting up a shady business here. Little Baptist church on the corner to the east, and the Metropolitan Methodist Church a block over to the west. It's a wonder he hasn't been struck down."

Hodgins laughed. "I doubt that's even crossed the broker's mind. Who are we visiting first?"

Henry checked his paper. "Mr. Miller."

They walked up the narrow lane and found the pawnbroker. The shop was dingy inside as little light made it through the filthy windows. A few lanterns had been set out, but they didn't help much. The walls were covered in shelving, buckling under the weight of the goods up for sale. Hodgins glanced at some of the tags, reading the dates written on them, indicating when the items arrived at the shop. Many items had been pawned years earlier and never reclaimed. At the back of the shop a frail-looking man watched every move they made. He was well protected behind the wooden counter.

"I think you could take this one," Hodgins whispered to Barnes. "He's in worse shape than you."

Barnes ignored the jibe and walked up to the broker.

"What can I help you with, Constable? I'm certain I have something that you can afford on your meagre salary."

"We're here on business. Looking for a stolen pocket watch."

Miller waved his wrinkled hands. "Don't deal in stolen goods. I'm an honest man, I am. Don't want no trouble."

"Have you had anyone come in over the past few days with a gold pocket watch? Has an engraving on the inside."

"No. Nothing like that. Look around. You'll see I don't deal in jewellery."

Hodgins joined Barnes at the back of the shop and nodded at the broker. "Morning, Jim. Didn't realize this was your place."

Miller nodded in response. "Detective. Had to move. Couldn't afford the rent. You know me. I'm telling ya, I ain't got a pocket watch. There's a new man on Millstone Lane. Pawnbroker and saloon keeper. He deals in jewellery. Don't care if the real owner brings it in, if you know what I mean." He tapped the side of his nose and winked.

"Thanks for the tip. We'll check him out. Don't suppose you have any umbrellas for sale?"

Miller smiled. "Special deal today. Anyone who come in before noon gets a free umbrella. Take your pick." He pointed to his left. "They're just on the other side of that table."

Hodgins thanked him again, and sent Barnes to pick two of the best umbrellas before they headed over to Millstone Lane.

The rain came down heavier and the wind had

picked up. By the time they finished the fifteen-minute walk they were drenched, only their heads remaining dry. Millstone Lane was a bit larger than the side street they just left, but no cheerier. They looked around the area before going to the pawnbroker's shop.

Barnes seemed puzzled. "Sir, the only thing on the lane is the back of the Osborne House Hotel."

"Take another look. There are a few small buildings towards the back. Pawn shop is probably in one of those. Get out that paper and tell me if this one's on your list. Miller said the owner is also a saloon keeper, so it makes sense there's a hotel here. Could be the barkeep."

"The rain smudged it. I think it's this one here. Kavanagh and Mur-something."

Hodgins started down the lane. "May as well see what's down here."

The building at the end of the lane had a small sign in the window–Kavanagh and Murphy, Pawn Brokers.

"Looks like this is the place." A small brass bell tinkled when Hodgins open the door.

Unlike Miller's shop, this one wasn't cluttered. A large counter lined the side wall with items neatly arranged on the shelving and tables. The man behind the counter stood several inches taller than Hodgins, and was twice as wide. A scar ran down his face from the corner of his left eye, disappearing under his chin. Where it went from there Hodgins couldn't tell as the man had little in the way of a neck. Hodgins looked at Barnes, glad he'd accompanied the lad.

Barnes entered behind him, but stopped just inside the door. His mouth gaped slightly as he stared at the giant shopkeeper.

Hodgins turned back towards the broker. "Are you Mr. Kavanagh?" He showed his badge.

"Nah. Whatcha want?" His voice was low and gravely.

"I'm trying to track a missing pocket watch." Hodgins looked at the items under the glass in the counter. "I see you have quite a selection of jewellery. By any chance has anyone come in lately looking to sell or pawn a gold pocket watch? There's an engraving on the inside cover."

The man moved in what Hodgins thought might be a shrug, but it was difficult to tell since the giant's head practically sat on his shoulders. "If ya ain't buying or selling, leave. Yur scaring off the punters."

Hodgins turned just in time to see someone hastily exit the shop. The site of Barnes' uniform was enough to scare anyone selling stolen goods.

"Would Mr. Kavanagh be at the Osborne by any chance?"

"Maybe."

It was obvious they weren't going to get any information from this man, and Hodgins didn't want to try strong-arming the hulk. They left and went into the hotel.

"May as well have an early lunch while we're here. Look, there's an empty table by the fire."

A server came over as soon as they sat. Hodgins took the opportunity to inquire about the pawnbroker.

"Does Mr. Kavanagh work at this hotel?"

She nodded. "That's him at the bar. What can I get you?"

Hodgins looked at Barnes. "Ploughman's?" Barnes nodded.

"Two Ploughman lunches, and a large pot of tea."

When she left, Barnes leaned back in the chair. "That chap was terrifying. I wouldn't want to get in a fight with him."

"Completely agree. At least Kavanagh looks less likely to start a fight." Hodgins positioned himself to watch the man.

Based on the height of the bar, Hodgins guessed Kavanagh to be around six feet tall. The bartender wore a dingy white shirt, with sleeve garters keeping the cuffs from getting soiled. A dark brown vest, unbuttoned, hid a few of the stains, but based on the ones Hodgins saw, the rest of his shirt and the apron around his waist likely matched the soiled shirt front. The red bow tie seemed to be the only item of clean clothing.

The bar was impressive. A wall of mirrors covered the area behind the bar, reflecting back any sunlight that made its way in. Kerosene ceiling fixtures also reflected light in the mirror. A few small shelves sat at either end of the mirror, displaying the higher priced liquor. There were even hooks at the front of the bar with white cleaning rags hanging from them.

Hodgins took in the rest of the room, looking for a possible back way out in case Kavanagh bolted. He couldn't see any obvious exits. Several large chandeliers hung from the ceiling with tables carefully placed so the wax from the candles wouldn't drip on the patrons. Not a high-class place, but not a dump either.

The server said something to Kavanagh and pointed at Hodgins before bringing over their pot of tea. Hodgins drank half a cup before going to speak with the bartender.

"Are you Mr. Kavanagh?" Hodgins pulled back his jacket to reveal his badge.

"What if I am?" Kavanagh wiped the bar counter without bothering to look up.

"I understand you own the pawn shop out back in Millstone Lane."

"Might."

Hodgins placed his hand on the cloth as it swiped past him. "I only want to ask you a few questions. Won't take but a minute. Your assistant wasn't very helpful." Hodgins placed extra emphasis on the word assistant.

Kavanagh actually laughed. "Assistant? Ya mean Murphy? We're business partners. He runs the shop and I handle the procurement of items with a higher value. Also loan out money. Murphy ain't too good with sums, but he can handle simple sales. I also have a stake in this place. We got no need for the likes of you. State your business and go back to your table." He tugged the cloth out from under Hodgins' hand.

"We're looking for a pocket watch that went missing. Possibly someone tried to sell it to you? I'm certain you wouldn't want to be caught with stolen merchandise. A simple gold watch and chain, with an engraving on the inside." Hodgins opened his notebook. "Says, *With hard work and dedication, anything is possible.* Have you seen anything like that?"

"Got lots of gold watches. Now, unless you plan on arresting me, which I know you ain't, I got work to do."

"Surprised the word work didn't get stuck in your throat."

Kavanagh snarled, dropped the rag on Hodgins' notebook, and went to take a customer's order.

Hodgins removed the rag, went back to the table, and topped up his tea. "Not going to get much out of him. Wouldn't surprise me if he's seen it. Not the most honest man. Money lender as well as pawning items. I know the type. Interest payments are more than the initial loan. It's a never-ending circle for those desperate enough to borrow from people like him.

"Why not have one of the lads come down, out of uniform, and have a look at the pocket watches in the case? You never know if we'll get lucky."

Hodgins nodded. "Not a bad idea, but not just yet. Now he knows we're looking for it, he'll probably put it away for a bit. We still have other shops to check out."

CHAPTER FOURTEEN

The rain stopped by the time they returned to the station. Both officers were weary and soaked. Hodgins dragged a chair over to the pot-belly stove against the back wall and sat with his feet propped up on the stove's fender.

"Has anyone heard from Harrington today?"

One of the constables came over with a large envelope. "He came in a short while ago on his way home and left this for you."

Hodgins took the contents out and read it. He jolted upright. "Barnes. My office."

The detective spread the papers across his desk. "Looks like he found the court record on the disagreement between Logan and Buckingham." He passed Barnes the pages one at a time, after reading them. "More than just a spat. Logan made it sound as though it was just a minor disagreement, but according to this, he was claiming ten acres of Buckingham's land was actually his."

Barnes whistled. "That much land is worth a fair bit. Who won?"

Hodgins read the next page. "Buckingham. But that's not all. Logan offered to purchase it, but for much less than it's worth. I wonder if he'll try to buy it from the son." He looked up. "Did you find out anything about a will?"

Barnes smacked his forehead. "I plum forgot. Was going to tell you when you got back. Mrs. Buckingham gave me the name of their lawyer and a note to instruct him to give me any information I needed. He had a short will. Left the land and house to his son, with the provision Mrs. Buckingham stay on the farm for the rest of her natural life. Left a few bits and bobs and one of the horses to his daughter. Even though much of the land wasn't being farmed, he actually owned almost a hundred acres." Barnes flipped open his notebook. "Ninety-five acres to be exact. Add that to the land Charlie owns and the son will be quite wealthy."

Hodgins nodded. "I'd say that's a pretty good reason for murder. Wouldn't be the first time a parent was killed for their money, or in this case, land. Has Riddell found out anything yet?"

"Haven't seen him since last evening. Probably still tracking down the man Charlie assaulted."

"Can't completely rule out anyone, yet. I'm going to see if I can find anything more about the son-in-law, McTaggart. Why don't you have a chat with Charlie and see if Logan has expressed interest in purchasing any of the land?"

* * *

Hodgins headed over to Parliament Street, where McTaggart used to have his chemist shop. Fortunately, it was a short walk from the station on Wilton Avenue and the rain had stopped. The building still stood vacant, but the neighbouring shopkeeper said someone was moving in next week.

"Did you know McTaggart well?

The stout shopkeeper smiled. "Yes, very pleasant man. Quite convenient having him here. His wife was very nice, too. She helped out most days. Stopped coming in after the commotion."

"Commotion? What happened?" Hodgins had his notebook out, ready.

She looked around to make sure no one was listening. "The most horrid man came in. They were shouting, but I couldn't make out what they said. A lot of items got broke. Beatrice was sweeping up the mess when I went in after the man left."

"Hmm, interesting. Did you recognize the man? An unhappy customer perhaps?"

"No. Ain't never seen him 'round here before, and I'd remember him. Scar down his face, and practically no neck."

The last comment got Hodgins attention. A scar and no neck. He knew one person who fit that description. "How long ago did this happen?"

"Let me think. Maybe a month before they moved. That man was back yesterday looking for them, but I told him I didn't know where they went, which is true enough. Left without a word."

Hodgins tipped his hat. "Thank you, ma'am. You've been most helpful."

He hurried back to the station, hoping that Barnes hadn't left yet. He arrived just at the young constable was heading out.

"Barnes, wait up. I'm coming with you."

"Sir? Have you found something?"

"McTaggart knew our friend with no neck. He's still in town, isn't he?"

"Yes. They're planning the funeral for tomorrow and he'll be going back to Kleinburg right after. His wife is staying with her mother a few weeks.

They headed to John Mitchell's livery on Duke Street. Hiring a buggy would be cheaper than taking a hansom cab all the way to the Buckingham farm. Hodgins drove the horse hard, and made good time. He handed Barnes the reins then jumped off, and Barnes continued on to the son's farm.

Hodgins listened to the sounds coming from the house before knocking. Pots rattled and something was being chopped in preparation of the evening meal. He raised his hand and rapped on the door. Mr. McTaggart answered.

"Sorry to interrupt, but I need to speak with you."

McTaggart seemed flustered. "I ... well ..." He glanced at his mother-in-law.

"Won't take long." Hodgins smiled, hoping to settle the man.

McTaggart hesitated, then joined Hodgins outside.

The detective made himself comfortable on the top step of the porch, notebook perched on his knee. McTaggart sat beside him.

"Are you in some sort of trouble?" Hodgins asked.

"Trouble? Why would you ask that?" He hung his head and fidgeted with his hands.

"One of your old neighbours on Parliament Street told me about an argument a month ago. I recognized the description of the man. He works at Kavanagh's pawn shop. Do you owe them money?"

McTaggart grabbed Hodgins' arm. "Please, you can't tell anyone. I placed a few bets on the dog races. Bad bets."

"Dog races? He operates a betting establishment? My, he certainly is a busy man. Pawning, money lending, and betting. How much do you owe?"

"Three hundred dollars. I can get half that if I sell the horse Bucky left Bea. But I can't pay the rest back. If he finds me …"

"Don't worry. I'm not interested in your gambling habits. As long as they're not tied up in Mr. Buckingham's death."

McTaggart looked shocked. "What? No. I'd never

do anything like that. How can you even think it?"

"Just doing my job. That's all I need to know, for now. I'll just look around the barn a bit while I wait for my constable to come back, if you don't have any objections."

"No objections. Maybe you'll find something. Thank you, Detective." McTaggart took a deep breath and plastered a smile on his face before entering the house.

Hodgins remained sitting and made a few notes before heading to the barn. Little had changed. Two horses occupied the stalls. Either no one was working the fields, or they were finished plowing. He walked over and patted the nose of old the draft horse.

"Don't suppose you know who did it? Maybe you can walk over and nudge the guilty person? Make my job a lot easier."

He gave each horse a handful of hay, then looked in the empty stalls again. The only thing that had changed was a new bird nest in the overalls. He thought about the boots he'd taken back to the station. They had to belong to someone, either a young person or a woman. No one lived on the farm except the

Buckinghams, and the boots didn't belong to any of the women. He thought back to his meeting with Peter Clark. He looked about the right size. Could either he or his brother have left them behind? No, probably not. They weren't employed long enough to have belongings on the farm.

He climbed into the loft and had a good look around. The litter of kittens was still up there, along with more hay. He climbed back down and walked the outside perimeter. Everything looked the same. Hodgins wandered through the garden when the clomping of hooves approached. Barnes had returned.

Hodgins scrambled into the buggy. "That was a quick trip."

"Most disagreeable young man. Told me to mind my own business and practically threw me off his property."

Hodgins looked to the west. "Sun's low. Better get back. Maybe Mr. Logan will be more forthcoming. Why don't you try to have a chat with him tomorrow."

* * *

Thirty minutes later, Hodgins dropped Barnes at the station, then returned the buggy himself and headed home. Scraps greeted him at the door, then tugged at the leash hanging on the hook. "Taking the dog out for a short walk," he called to his wife. He fastened the leash and took the dog around the block. The rain left a chill in the air along with numerous puddles. Scraps found every one, distracting Hodgins' thoughts.

Normally, quiet time with Scraps helped him put the facts together, but tonight it wasn't working. Despite the dog's protests, they were back home in less than an hour. He put Scraps in the backyard with Sara and her cousins, then set the table while Cordelia finished up the last of the cooking.

"Thought I might have a lead, but so far it's gone nowhere. The son-in-law's in debit with bad gambling bets. The person looking for him isn't someone I'd want after me. He swears he had nothing to do with Bucky's murder, and I believe him."

"You'll need a few more plates. Jonathan and Elizabeth are joining us, then taking their children back home. Dinner will be another half hour. Why don't you check on the twins? They should be waking soon."

Hodgins added the extra place settings, then went upstairs, returning a few minutes later. "They're awake.

I've put them in their playpen in the front room for now. I'm glad my brother is working things out with his wife. It's nice having him back in the city. His business is picking up nicely and it shouldn't take long to establish himself."

Cordelia finished chopping the vegetables then put them on to cook. "Sara enjoys having her cousins here. They're getting along nicely. And, of course, the dog enjoys the extra attention. Oh, I spoke with mother about needing a nanny and didn't even have to discourage her. She admits she doesn't have the energy to help full time. Tomorrow, I plan on speaking with Violet to see if any of her friends would be suitable."

"Speaking of Violet, Henry doesn't have a ring yet. Don't think he has any idea what to buy."

"If he needs help picking one out, I can make a suggestion or two."

The back door slammed as the children raced in. Cordelia almost dropped a pot. "Slow down. The twins are in the front room and they're quiet for once. Go up and change. Your parents will be here shortly. You too, Sara. Hurry."

* * *

Dinner with the family was pleasant. Jonathan spoke of his new home and business. Even mentioned getting a dog after they've settled in. Just as Cordelia doled out the pudding, someone knocked on the front door. Hodgins went to answer it, but Scraps beat him to it. The dog's tail wagged and he barked continually.

"Must be Barnes," Hodgins called back as he walked down the hallway. He opened the door and Scraps immediately leapt up on the young constable. He was still in uniform.

"What brings you here this late? Isn't your shift over?" Hodgins stood back so Barnes could enter.

"Sara, come get the dog, will you?" Hodgins ushered Barnes into the front room and they both almost tripped over the excited dog. "Sara!"

"Coming, Papa." Sara raced in and dragged the dog into the kitchen.

"Sit, Henry. That look on your face tells me there's been trouble."

Rather than sitting, Barnes chose to lean on the fireplace mantle. "There's been another murder, and I have a feeling it's somehow connected to the Buckinghams."

CHAPTER FIFTEEN

"Blast. Who is it this time? Please don't tell me Mrs. Buckingham's been killed. One elderly person murdered is more than enough."

Henry flipped open his notebook. "No, this time it's a man in his forties. Been identified as Gordon Murphy."

Hodgins interrupted. "Why is that name familiar?"

"Scar down the right side of his face, and no neck. Remember the pawn brokers? Kavanagh and Murphy?"

Hodgins nodded. "Murphy. And I just found out today that McTaggart owes Murphy three hundred dollars. Coincidence? I wonder if McTaggart was scared enough to make sure the debt was never collected? Tomorrow's the funeral. I believe you said McTaggart planned on going back to Kleinburg after it was over?"

Barnes closed his notebook. "That's what he told me. Buckingham was a popular enough fellow. Should be something in the paper about the service. St. James Cemetery would be closest to their farm."

"Already know they plan on a farm burial. I'll find when it will be and pull McTaggart aside afterwards." Hodgins smacked his forehead. "Where are my manners? You probably haven't eaten, and we have plenty. Join us?"

"Thank you, sir, but I'm expected at the Halloway's."

Barnes left and Hodgins grabbed the newspaper from the side table. The obituaries were listed on page two. He found the one for Buckingham.

In this city, on the 3rd of May Elmer Buckingham, in his 78th year. Funeral tomorrow, 12th of May, at 2 o'clock. Interment to be on the family farm. Friends and acquaintances are invited to attend.

He jotted the information in his notebook, dropped the newspaper back on the side table, then joined his family in the kitchen. "I'll need my good suit pressed. Have to attend a funeral tomorrow afternoon."

Cordelia placed a bowl of plum pudding in front of him. "Henry came here just to tell you about a funeral"?

"No. There's been another murder." Hodgins grinned as his sister-in-law blanched.

* * *

When Hodgins arrived at Station Four the next morning, he checked the train schedule. The next one for Kleinburg didn't leave until 5:00 p.m. McTaggart would have to go straight from the funeral if he hoped to catch it. Hodgins would make certain to delay the man.

It turned out to be an uneventful morning. None of his constables had anything new to report and Hodgins couldn't come up with even one new lead to check.

He headed home for lunch, then changed into his Sunday suit and hired a cabriolet to take him to the funeral. Farmers from across the city attended, always saddened to see one of their own die, even if they didn't know him. School mates of Charlie and Beatrice and friends of Mrs. Buckingham from her church societies added to the gathering. Hodgins stayed towards the back, keeping out of the way but watching McTaggart. He was ready when the man headed out.

"Mr. McTaggart, might I have a word?"

"I'm in rather a hurry." He checked his pocket watch. "Barely enough time to catch my train."

"I'm afraid you won't be going anywhere tonight. Mr. Murphy has been murdered."

McTaggart looked puzzled. "Murphy? I don't know any Murphy."

"Yes, you do. You told me as much yesterday. You owe him a lot of money. Very convenient that he's dead and your debt might possibly be buried with him. Unless, of course, his associate comes collecting."

McTaggart's jaw dropped and he stared at the detective. Hodgins could see him processing the insinuation.

"You can't think I did it?"

Hodgins leaned against a tree. "Well, I don't know what to think. Not yet. Yesterday, you were extremely worried that your family would find out you owed so much money. Even the sale of your wife's newly inherited horse would only cover half your debt. Next day I find out the man you owe money to is dead. If you were me, what would you think?"

"But I was here at the farm. All day. Ask anyone."

"I don't think today is a good day to question your wife and mother-in-law, do you?"

McTaggart nodded. "What will I tell them?"

Hodgins shrugged. "Tell them you had a change of heart. Couldn't leave your wife the same day you buried her father. I'll be out in the morning, and there'll be a constable at the station tomorrow to make certain you don't take the early train."

"Detective." Hodgins turned to see Mrs. McTaggart crossing the lawn towards them. "So nice of you to attend my father's funeral. Have you made any arrests yet?"

"We're still following leads. I'll be back out in the morning. I have a few more inquires."

"Of course. Anything to help find the monster who killed Papa." She turned to her husband. "Won't you be late for the train?"

"Changed my mind. It's been a stressful day for you and your mother. I'll take the train tomorrow evening. There's nothing pressing that can't wait another day." He turned to Hodgins. "If you'll excuse us." He took his wife's arm and led her towards the house.

* * *

When Hodgins arrived back at his desk, a file lay waiting for him. Dr. Stonehouse had finally made a copy of the report on Buckingham's autopsy. The pitchfork had been used to try to mask the bullet hole, but the bullet stayed inside the body. The coroner confirmed it was a .22 caliber. Unfortunately, a common size shot, owned by many. Hodgins tucked the file into a drawer and headed to the coroner's.

"Afternoon, Dr. Stonehouse. Have you had a chance to look at the new victim, Murphy?"

"Not yet. All I can tell you is he was shot. Won't have time to give him a thorough going over until tomorrow."

"Tomorrow's soon enough. At least I have a suspect for that one."

CHAPTER SIXTEEN

Hodgins went back to work and assigned one of the more senior constables to keep an eye at the train station the next morning. Shame to waste a seasoned officer, but he couldn't risk one of the newer recruits making a mistake or simply being too afraid or unsure what to do if McTaggart did make a break for it.

He made a cup of tea and went back into his office to review his notes, stopping when he came to the short interview with the youngest Clark brother. Lad hadn't even given his first name. Hodgins tapped the paper with his pencil, pondering what to do.

Go back out to the Clark house? No, not wise. This lad didn't seem to be as bad as the others. Mr. Clark would take a strip off his hide if he found out one of his sons tried to turn in his brothers. But, he mentioned they had a gun. Could it be the one he was looking for?

Peter or John couldn't have shot Bucky from Elora. No, they were definitely off the suspect list. Hodgins needed to find the killer, but at the expense of a boy of, what, twelve? Since his brothers couldn't have done it, Hodgins decided to let the boy be.

He asked one of the constables for the report on Murphy. It couldn't be a coincidence that McTaggart's name was linked with both murders. Did he kill his father-in-law in the hopes of inheriting enough to get him out of debt, then kill the unscrupulous money lender when the inheritance turned out to be a pittance?

Richardson knocked on the door frame before entering. "Here it is, sir. Not much information yet."

"Thank you. Hopefully we can solve it before the file gets too fat. Is Riddell about?"

"No. He was looking through the old files, then yelled *Eureka* and ran out the door. Didn't say where he was going."

Hodgins chuckled. "Eureka, eh? Must have found something good. Is the file still on his desk?"

"Yes. I'll get it." Richardson turned to leave Hodgins' office.

"Never mind. I'll go have a look at it. If the files are gathered, then I won't know what he saw. Haven't seen Barnes, have you?"

"Called out to a minor disturbance over at Allan Gardens. Seems someone had too much to drink and began pulling out the flowers. Been gone about an hour. Should be back soon I expect."

Both turned at a disturbance at the front entrance. "Looks like Barnes corralled his drunk."

Barnes deposited the man on a bench just inside the door. The drunk immediately fell on his side and started snoring.

"Horticultural Society isn't pressing charges. They just wanted him off the property so they could start repairing the damage. Shall I lock him up until he's sober? He had a wallet and his address is in it."

Hodgins waved Richardson over. "Take our guest to the cells until he's sober, then call on the address. Maybe someone will claim him. Barnes, join me at Riddell's desk and see if we can figure out why he left so suddenly."

Richardson roused the drunk while Hodgins and Barnes checked the papers spewed about Riddell's desk top.

"What are we looking for?" Barnes asked.

"Haven't a clue. Richardson said Riddell yelled *Eureka* then ran out the door. Hopefully what it was will be obvious. All these reports are complaints against Charlie Buckingham. Maybe Riddell's gone off to his farm to confront him about … what?"

Barnes reached for a page, but Hodgins grabbed his arm. "Don't move anything. This is how they were arranged when he shot off. If we know where he was standing, maybe we can narrow it down."

Hodgins called out to everyone in the room. "Did anyone see exactly where Riddell was before he ran out? The exact spot."

Everyone shook their head or shrugged their shoulders.

"Only looked up when he yelled, and he was moving by then," one answered.

"Blast! Riddell knew Charlie somewhat. He may have noticed something that wouldn't mean anything to us."

Barnes touched Hodgins' arm. "Sir, Richardson's back. Maybe he saw."

Hodgins looked up. "Richardson. Did you see where Riddell stood before he hollered?"

"Yes, sir. I was at the desk right opposite. He was looking at a paper at this end of the desk." Richardson pointed to the right of where Hodgins stood.

Hodgins mumbled his thanks and picked up the only page at that end of the desk. He read for a moment, then whistled. He handed the page to Barnes. "Look at this."

"Oh, my. Which farm do we go to?"

Hodgins thought a moment. "Both if necessary. We'll grab the first cab and head to the senior Buckingham's. If Riddell isn't there, we'll continue on to Charlie's farm."

* * *

The sun had almost set by the time they tracked Riddell down at Charlie's farm. Loud voices accompanied by the sound of breaking wood came from inside the house. A woman screamed.

"Wait here," Hodgins told the driver as he leapt out of the cabriolet. The horse stomped and took a few steps back as another loud crash echoed inside.

Barnes got to the door before Hodgins, and

entered without knocking. Mrs. Buckingham sat on the floor in the corner, still screaming. Charlie and Riddell were locked hand to fist, dancing around broken kitchen chairs.

"Barnes, get her out of here." Hodgins ran over to try and separate the fighting men. "Tell the driver to take you to her in-laws, then come back here. She's too hysterical to go on her own."

Hodgins kicked the broken chairs out of the way and reached for Riddell to pull him away. Charlie's fist flew and caught Hodgins square in the eye. The two fighters rolled close to the fireplace. Hodgins briefly contemplated letting them get scorched, then realized they may spread the fire throughout the house. He looked around for anything heavy. A wrought iron frying pan hung over kitchen counter. Hodgins grabbed it and brought it down on Charlie's back. The fighting stopped.

Hodgins grabbed Riddell and practically threw him onto one of the two undamaged chairs. "What were you thinking? He'll probably file charges against you."

"Do you know what he did? He's a monster. I tried to arrest him but—"

Hodgins softened a little, and placed a hand on Riddell's shoulder. "I saw the report. Don't know why someone hadn't mentioned it before. Embarrassed I suppose. How do you tell the coppers your son struck his father? If his sister hadn't filed the report we wouldn't know."

"But why would she withdraw the complaint?" Riddell wiped his mouth, the back of his hand coming away red.

Hodgins found a cloth and wet it so Riddell could clean his wounds. Charlie moaned and tried to get up. Hodgins helped him into the only other unbroken chair and found another cloth for him.

"Let's call it a draw, shall we gentlemen?"

"I'll have your badge for this." Charlie tried to stand, but Hodgins pushed him back into the chair then leaned against the counter. "Let's be reasonable. The only witness to the fight is your wife, and she's too hysterical to tell us much. Riddell tried to arrest you, you resisted. He was within the law to restrain you. With your record, I don't think a judge would believe you if you said Riddell started it."

Charlie looked around. "Where's Adelia?"

"Constable Barnes took her to your mother's. When he returns, what's say we all go over there?" Hodgins looked around. "While we're waiting, how about we clean up this mess? No need to leave it for your wife."

"Tidying up is women's work." Charlie crossed his arms and glared at Hodgins.

"You made this mess. You can damn well clean it up." Hodgins grabbed Charlie's collar and pulled him out of the chair. "Start with the debris from the chairs."

Hodgins tried to glare back, but even the smallest movement of his face throbbed.

By the time Barnes returned, the room looked a little less like a fight-ring and more like a kitchen. Hodgins sent Barnes back to the senior Buckingham's farm with Riddell, and had Charlie accompany him in the cabriolet. The driver seemed unconcerned with all the fighting. Probably used to it.

The ride back was quiet. Charlie sat stewing, and Hodgins had given up trying to engage the driver in conversation.

When they arrived, everyone sat in the kitchen. Adelia had gone from hysterical to angry. Her comments filled the house. "I can't believe he could behave like that. He should be locked up."

Riddell looked at Hodgins. "Guess I'm in for it now."

Charlie smirked. "Guess my complaint won't be dismissed after all. They'll believe my wife." He strolled into the kitchen and put his arm around her shoulders.

"Get away from me. If I'd known what you did, I never would have married you." She turned and pushed him away.

Charlie's face reddened. "Why you ungrateful little bitch." He lunged at her, but McTaggart grabbed him.

The three officers raced over. Hodgins asked Riddell for his handcuffs. "Charlie Buckingham, I'm arresting you for the murder of your father."

"But I didn't do it." Charlie struggled to get away from McTaggart while Hodgins tried to get the cuffs on.

His mother fainted, banging her head on the wood stove as she fell. Blood spread across the hardwood floor.

"Mother!"

CHAPTER SEVENTEEN

Beatrice knelt beside her mother's unconscious body, weeping. "Mother, please don't die."

"Damn! We need to get her to a doctor right away. Barnes, you take Charlie back in the cabriolet. That buggy will only hold two. I'll go with Riddell and we'll take Mrs. Buckingham with us."

He turned to Riddell. "Good thing you hired a brougham carriage. Plenty of room for the three of us. Tell the driver we'll be stopping at Toronto General on the way."

Barnes led a protesting Charlie out and Hodgins, Riddell, and McTaggart carried Mrs. Buckingham to the brougham. They gently set her on the back seat.

Beatrice climbed in and nestled her mother's head in her lap. "I'm coming with you."

"I'll hook up the buggy and follow," Mr. McTaggart said.

* * *

Hodgins stayed at the hospital until a doctor was able to check Mrs. Buckingham over. The injury wasn't deep, but it was serious for a woman of her advanced years. When he and Riddell arrived back at the station, Charlie had already been put in a cell. His yells were loud enough to reach the front of the station house.

"Riddell, my office." Hodgins paced behind his desk.

"Sir."

Hodgins came around and closed the door. It didn't buffer the sound much. "Don't you ever run off like that again. It was a careless and stupid thing to do. Anything could have happened. Always take another officer with you. You're just fortunate his wife is on your side. I'm putting an official reprimand in your file. Thank your lucky stars I'm not suspending you. It's late. Go home and have a good think about what you did."

Riddell hung his head. "Yes, sir."

"Now."

Riddell scrambled out of the chair and through detective's office door, bumping into Barnes along the way. Hodgins followed, but not quite so fast.

"Go home Barnes. It's late."

"Actually, I'm off to Violet's. Mind if I walk with you?" The two men set out on foot.

"Funny about Charlie," Hodgins said.

"Do you really believe he murdered his own father?"

"Difficult to say. He certainly didn't get along with him."

Barnes agreed. "The way he was fighting with Riddell. And with his wife right there in the room."

"Never mind Charlie. It was Riddell's fighting that has my blood boiling. Almost suspended him. Gave him a good tongue lashing. I expect everyone within twenty feet of my office heard it. Can't have my constables running off like that. Always have backup. You just never know what you'll run into."

"Yes, sir. What about that money lender? Are the two murders connected?"

"I thought so, but now I'm not at all certain. I had McTaggart pegged for both. My theory was he murder his father-in-law for any inheritance left to his wife. When it wasn't enough to cover the loan, he just murdered Murphy, hoping to erase the debt."

Barnes nodded. "That sounds reasonable. Charlie complained all the way to the station that he was being arrested unfairly. Not exactly his words, but I don't care for that kind of language. He was still carrying on when I left him in the cell. Expect his lawyer will get him out shortly."

Hodgins laughed. "I can well imagine the language. Probably sounded more like a dock worker than a farmer. Maybe the two murders aren't connected. Charlie killed his father and McTaggart killed Murphy. How do we prove either?"

"I wish I knew, sir."

They turned up Yonge Street, enjoying the quiet of the early evening. The shops had long since closed and few buggies travelled the roads in the dark. The sky was clear and the full moon had just started to wane so it helped illuminate the way. Neither spoke for several blocks. They crossed over Yorkville Avenue and Hodgins stopped suddenly.

"Missed the turn." They backtracked a few feet and continued west on Yorkville to Avenue Road. They were almost at Hodgins' house and heard Scraps' barking, the sound carrying down the quiet street.

"Sara must have left the dog out alone again. Wonder the neighbours don't complain."

"The Halloways don't mind him," Barnes said.

"But the other neighbours aren't dog lovers. Enjoy your evening."

Barnes continued to his sweetheart's home next door, and Hodgins went around to the back of his house. Scraps stopped barking and ran over to the gate.

"Good boy." He patted the dog's head then went into the back porch, Scraps close on his heels.

From the look of the dirty plates in the sink, his wife and daughter hadn't waited dinner for him. Cordelia stood with her hands on her hips when he walked in. "Well, it's about time. Sara's already in bed. Sit. Your supper's warming."

She cleared the lone clean plate off the table and went to the wood stove to dole out his meal. Hodgins took the plate from her. "No, you sit and enjoy a cup of tea. I can get my own supper."

He lifted the lid off the post and inhaled. "Ah. Irish stew. Just what I need." He sat at the table beside her and Scraps curled up on his rug by the stove.

"Tell me, what kept you so late?" Cordelia was more curious than angry. Keeping supper warm was not unusual when her husband worked a murder case.

Hodgins took a few mouthfuls of food before answering. "One of my constables went off half-cocked to confront a suspect, on his own of all things. I grabbed Barnes and we went off after him. Found my constable rolling around the floor with the suspect."

"From the look of that eye, I'd say you joined them."

"Hmm, what? Oh, forgot about that. Got that trying to separate them. I'll put ice on it later." He took a few more bites before continuing. "His wife was in hysterics, so I sent Barnes to take her to her in-laws. When he came back, we all went over. One thing led to another, and his mother fainted, banging her head. Had to take her to the hospital."

"My word, you've had a busy evening. What caused her to faint?"

"We arrested her son for killing his father."

Cordelia's cup clattered as it hit the saucer. "Goodness. Is she going to be all right?"

Hodgins shrugged. "If she was several years

younger, probably. But she's in her seventies. Any bang on the head is serious. She was still unconscious when I left the family at the hospital."

"Do you really believe he killed his own father?"

Hodgins scooped more of the delicious stew into his mouth before answering, giving him a little time to think. "Honestly? I don't know. He says he didn't, but they all do, don't they? Riddell found an old complaint his sister filed after he assaulted his father years ago. She withdrew it, so nothing came of it. Must have made for some pretty hard feelings within the family though. Meant to ask why she didn't follow through, but with her mother's fall, it slipped my mind."

Hodgins ate the last mouthful and his stomach grumbled. Cordelia took the plate to the wood stove and refilled it.

"You seem exceptionally hungry tonight."

"Haven't eaten since breakfast. Didn't realize just how famished I am."

Cordelia refilled both their tea cups then sat again. "I'm not surprised she withdrew the complaint. It is her brother after all. I'd guess that her mother pressured her to do it. No matter what your children do, they're still your children. They'd have to do a lot worse for you to turn your back on them."

Hodgins nodded. "You mean like murder their own kin?"

"Exactly."

Hodgins dug into his second helping. "It's nice to sit and chat without the children running around or crying. I'm glad Jonathan's brood are back home, much as I enjoyed having them. Won't be long before the twins are running around. I might just have to work late more often so we can have time to ourselves."

"Don't you dare even think that. But I agree. Time alone will be precious for the next several years. Have you made any progress on the other murder? You thought they were connected."

Hodgins finished the second helping of stew then pushed the plate away. "Going to have to re-think that one. If Charlie killed his father, and not McTaggart, then we have two murderers on our hands. McTaggart has no history of violence we've been able to find. Totally out of character for him to commit one, never mind two, murders. I've ruled out those Clark brothers for both murders, but I don't want to stop looking just because we have someone in jail."

"How long can you hold him?"

"Without any evidence, not long. As Barnes commented to me earlier, a lawyer will probably have him out by morning."

Cordelia cleared away the dishes. "Have you found the gun that killed them?"

"No. Haven't got the coroner's report on Murphy yet, so I don't even know if we're looking for the same weapon.

* * *

Next morning when Hodgins arrived at Station House Four, all the constables and sergeants crowded around one of the desks.

"Having a party and didn't invite me?" he joked.

The men parted and a very embarrassed Harrington appeared, seated at Barnes' desk.

"Doctor gave him the go-ahead to work full days, desk work only," Barnes said.

Hodgins joined the crowd, a huge smile plastered on his face. "Well it's about time. How you feeling lad? You certain you're ready to return to work?"

"I'm fine, thank you sir. As long as I stay off my

feet, that is. Guess I'll be doing everyone's paperwork for a while."

A cheer rose from the officers.

"Not so fast. I've got something special for him to do. Barnes, can you assist him over to the registry office to go over those land records again? If Harrington's going to be on his backside, he can sit over there. He'll probably get more accomplished on his rump than most of you lot will on your feet all day."

The men groaned at Hodgins' comment, and one by one went back to their desk's or out on the beat. Barnes went outside and hailed the first hansom cab that came by, then helped Harrington down the stairs and into the cab.

"Riddell, join me in my office."

"What'd ya do this time, Tom?" one of the constables teased.

"Dammed if I know. Guess I'll find out." Riddell grabbed his notebook then edged into Hodgins' office.

"Don't look so worried, lad. Just want to talk to you about Charlie. Do you really believe he killed his own father? The report his sister filed years ago doesn't say what the fight was about, and I didn't get a chance to ask yesterday. Please, leave your personal feelings out of it."

Riddell thought for a moment. "Honestly, I don't know. I've never seen the good side of him, and my brother was afraid of him. Never heard tell of anyone saying a good word about him. Yes, he's more than capable of assault, but I don't know how far he'd take it. I'll look into it. I know I've made a mess of things and I'd like the opportunity to make it up. I'll stop at the hospital and see how Mrs. Buckingham is, and talk to the McTaggarts. I'm certain Beatrice will answer my questions."

Hodgins nodded. "Good lad. Clean up the mess and I'll add a note to the file to say you've made amends. Then we won't dwell on it further. If you take care of the Buckinghams, I can concentrate on McTaggart and the Murphy murder. At least he won't be leaving town so soon now that his mother-in-law is in the hospital."

"Thank you, sir." Riddell scrambled out of Hodgins' office and headed out the front door.

Hodgins flipped through the files on the edge of his desk, looking to see if the report on Murphy had been delivered. Dr. Stonehouse came in just as he was searching.

"Bad time, detective?"

Hodgins looked up. "No, not at all. Come in."

"I've finished the autopsy on Murphy. The bullet was a bit damaged, but it was clearly the same as the one that came out of Buckingham. Here's a copy of my report."

"So, we're looking for one person for both murders then."

Stonehouse leaned back in the chair and crossed his legs. "Not my call, but I'd agree. As I said before, a common enough gun, and many 'round here would have one of that caliber. Any leads?"

"I do have one person that has a motive for both, albeit the motive for killing Mr. Buckingham is small, and totally out of character from what I can tell. I'll need to look into that a bit more. Too bad there wasn't an easy way for us to look up old files. Push a button and voila." Hodgins shrugged. "Maybe someday."

He grinned as he looked over at the new coroner, who sat quite relaxed and seemed in no hurry to leave. Dr. McKenzie had always been in rush. Hand over the information and back to his own office.

"Would you like a cup of tea, doctor?"

"Thank you, but no. I should be getting back to work. Another time?"

"By all means. Once this is all cleared up, we'll definitely have to have you over for a meal. Bring a friend if you like."

Stonehouse rose to leave. "As you know, I'm not married, and I've had no time to acquire friends, lady friends in particular. Unlike some, I'm not adverse to having someone make arrangements."

Hodgins laughed. "I see. I'll ask my wife if she knows of anyone suitable." He reached over his desk and shook the coroner's hand. "Cordelia will know one or two young ladies that would make for a proper companion. Of that I have no doubt."

Hodgins accompanied Stonehouse out and went back to the files. The McTaggarts moved recently, so he started there. Maybe the chemist relocated for reasons other than running from a bad debt.

He spent the morning reading reports and found nothing on McTaggart. Needing to give his eyes a break, he decided to head to the records office and see how Harrington was getting on.

A typical spring day greeted him, sunny with a slight breeze, so Hodgins decided to walk. He passed Barnes on his beat and stopped to chat briefly.

"Got Harrington all settled then?"

"Yes, sir. He's happy to be doing anything, even going through the dusty records. Seems he was getting restless at home. His mother fussed something terrible. Glad to be back full time, even if he can't walk the beat."

"I know how that is. Just going to see how he's getting on. Riddell is following up with the Buckinghams to find out why the assault report was withdrawn, and see how Mrs. Buckingham is doing. Tomorrow morning, I want the three of you in my office so we can review our notes. Maybe something will jump out at one of us."

"Yes, sir. I'll make sure everyone is there."

Hodgins continued on and found Harrington leaning over a large record book in an unnaturally quiet room. He dragged a chair over to sit with him. Every head turned at the grating sound. He leaned close so he could whisper without causing a fuss.

"How's it going, lad? Find anything useful?"

"Just one thing. A new entry two days ago. That land Mr. Buckingham and Mr. Logan disagreed over? Seems Logan just purchased it from the son. He didn't even wait for the old man to be buried." Harrington reached for a smaller record book that sat off to the side and opened it.

"Here it is."

CHAPTER EIGHTEEN

Hodgins stood to get a better look at the entry. "Well, that is interesting. I'm no expert, but it looks like he paid a fair price for it." He took out his notebook and wrote down all the details. "Guess I need to chat with Mr. Logan. Good work, Harrington. Ready to go back to the station?"

"No, I think I'll stay a little longer. See what else I can find. If I go back, the lads will just give me all their paperwork to do."

Hodgins slapped him on the back. "You're right about that. They'll take advantage of your injury. Why don't you look into the property that McTaggart vacated." He flipped through his notes and wrote out the address for Harrington.

"I'll make sure Barnes comes back to get you around noon. Can't have you starving."

"Thank you, sir."

Hodgins grabbed the first hansom cab he found and headed out to the Logan farm, asking the driver to wait. Mrs. Logan directed him to the barn then invited the driver in for tea. Logan was saddling up one of the horses.

"Mr. Logan. Might I have a word?"

"Just on my way to check on a few things." He glanced up at the detective. "Nothing that can't wait. What can I do for you, detective?"

"I understand you've recently expanded your farm."

Logan appeared startled and let go of the reins. "Y-yes. That's not against the law."

"Not at all. It is a little convenient that you purchased the very land you fought over with Mr. Buckingham, and only days after he was murdered. You can see how that looks."

Logan puffed out his substantial chest. "Now hold on. You're not accusing me of murder, are you?"

"No. Not yet anyway. Why the rush to purchase the land?"

Logan sat on a bale of hay. "Charlie came to me. Said he needed money and wanted to know if I was interested in that piece of property. Of course I jumped at the chance. He was offering a good price. Not a steal exactly, but very reasonable. I couldn't say no."

Hodgins made a few notes. "He needed money? Did he say what for?"

Logan shook his head. "No, and I wasn't about to ask. That man has a bad temper and I didn't want to be on the receiving end of it. Might have jeopardized the sale."

Hodgins touched his eye. "The man has a strong right hook."

He made a few notes and thanked Logan for his time. On the way back, he reviewed their conversation. He didn't get the impression Logan had lied. Actually seemed a little embarrassed to have been discovered purchasing the property so soon after Buckingham's death.

Hodgins found it interesting that Charlie needed money. Was that a lie to cover up something, or did Buckingham's son really need the cash? He'd have to look into that once he returned to the station house. And McTaggart was desperate for money. Could Charlie have fallen into the same problem? Did he gamble and lose? Maybe a much-needed loan that he couldn't pay back? Could it be possible that not one but two of his suspects had reason to murder both Buckingham and Murphy?

* * *

Hodgins arrived back at the station about an hour and a half after leaving it, a multitude of notes added to his notebook. Barnes stood at a table going through a large stack of newspapers.

"Barnes, can you join me in my office? And bring some tea, if you don't mind."

Hodgins settled behind his desk and pulled out the pad of foolscap that he'd been merging all their notes on to. Barnes came in a few minutes later carrying a small wooden tray covered in knicks and stains. Two mugs of tea and a plate of biscuits sat on it.

"Sergeant's wife sent these in with him. Don't know how these two managed to survive the day. They're quite delicious."

"Good lad. What are you looking for in all those newspapers?" Hodgins took a sip of tea then a bite of biscuit, nodding his approval.

"Not really sure. I thought I might find something

of interest. You know, all sorts of things are reported these days. Even unsubstantiated gossip. I'm at a loss where to look or for what."

"Well then, I have a task for you, unless you'd rather keep reading old news."

Barnes slid to the edge of his chair, pencil poised over his notebook. "A new task? That would be most welcome."

Hodgins smiled. "I just came back from the Logan farm. Said Charlie approached him right after his father was murdered to see if Logan still wanted to purchase that piece of land they squabbled over. Also mentioned Charlie needed money, but didn't say what for. Can you look into the young Mr. Buckingham's finances? Did he overspend, gamble, maybe kept a companion on the side?"

Barnes was just taking a sip of tea, and spit it out at that last comment. "A companion? Must be someone mighty desperate to take up with the likes of him. I'm amazed his wife is still with him."

"I agree. Just tossing thoughts out. If he really does owe money, he either has bad gambling debts, or overspent with the upkeep on his farm. You see what you can find out. I'm going to have a chat with Kavanagh. It's a long-shot but maybe both Charlie and his brother-in-law dealt with the pawn brokers. Also want to find out if the debt McTaggart had was with Murphy alone, or the business. If the business, then Kavanagh will be wanting to collect. Murphy's death won't have any effect on the loan."

Barnes stood, but didn't leave. "What about those Clark brothers?"

Hodgins waved his hand to dismiss the question. "They were still in Elora at the time and wouldn't have been able to kill Murphy. Their uncle confirmed they arrived the same day Buckingham was murdered. Damn train ride took all day. No way they're guilty, at least not for that. I've no doubt their younger brother was correct with what he saw and overheard, but it must be some other incident. Possibly the ruckus they caused the day before."

"I'll look into Charlie's finances right away." Barnes gulped down his tea, leaving the last biscuit for Hodgins before hurrying out.

Hodgins called after him. "Don't forget to gather Harrington from the Records Office." He added the most recent notes to the long list of comments before heading down to chat with Kavanagh. Unfortunately, the man wasn't behind the bar. Hodgins approached the server.

"Excuse me, I'm looking for Kavanagh." He flashed his badge.

"Don't need to flash that around. I 'member ya. Kavanagh ain't in. And no, I don't got no idea where he's off to." She turned her back on Hodgins and wiped the table with a dirty, wet rag.

Hodgins figured he must be at the pawn shop, so he went around to the back alley. A closed sign hung in the door window, but someone moved around inside. Hodgins rapped on the window.

A muffle voice yelled out. "Can't ya read. We're closed today."

"Toronto Constabulary."

The figure made its way toward the door, and Hodgins saw Kavanagh. The lock clicked, and the door opened a few inches.

"Told the police everything I know about Murphy's death. I weren't here and didn't see nothing. I got work to do." He started to close the door, but

Hodgins pushed back with his hand.

"It's not his murder I'm here about. Not directly anyway." He pushed the door open far enough to walk in. Kavanagh backtracked.

"Whadda ya want then?" Kavanagh seemed interested, but the way he narrowed his eyes told Hodgins he was either suspicious or hiding something.

"I'm curious about the workings of your business. Specifically, your loans and bets."

Kavanagh laughed. "Can't make due on a copper's salary? Need a bit of extra dosh?"

Hodgins smiled. "No, but thank you for the offer. Are they part of this business, or were they made between Murphy and the customer? Do the loans default to your establishment?"

"Depends. Which loan are you asking about?"

"Joseph McTaggart. I believe he owes around three hundred dollars. Will the debt revert to you or just vanish?" Hodgins snapped his fingers. "Poof. Free and clear."

"Ah, yes. That was a bet, not a loan. Murphy had that side business himself. Nothing to do with me. Anyone who owed money from the dogs are off the hook."

"Interesting." Hodgins took out his notebook and made notes. "Don't suppose you know if Charlie Buckingham bet on the dogs, or maybe had a loan with you?"

"Loan. Some of the punters I remember easily. That's one's a nasty piece of work. Owes a fair bit. Ain't got time to check."

"I'm sure my men will have ample time to see if you have any stolen items in your shop. Have to close you down to check, of course."

Kavanagh scowled, mumbling several words worthy of a dock worker before agreeing to look at his books.

Hodgins followed Kavanagh to the counter at the back and watched as he pulled a ledger book from underneath. Kavanagh ran his fingers down the column and flipped the page. "Here it is." Kavanagh whistled. "Didn't realize it got that high. Let me see."

He did some calculations in his head, fingers adding imaginary numbers in the air. "With interest, it's up to almost three thousand. I'm gonna have to have a chat with him."

"So am I," Hodgins mumbled. "Thank you for your time. Sorry for your loss."

"Loss? Oh, Murphy. Ya, thanks."

Hodgins walked back to the station house, trying to figure out how to prove Charlie murdered both his father and the pawn broker. He stopped at the coroner's office to see if Dr. Stonehouse could tell him anything about the weapon that killed Murphy.

The doctor looked up from his microscope when he heard the door open.

Hodgins nodded. "Sorry to interrupt, but I hoped you had more information on the gun from the second murder."

"Yes. Interesting thing about that. Was just about to head over and tell you about it. You've saved me a walk." Stonehouse handed a piece of paper to Hodgins. "It's all in there. Let me show you."

The doctor picked up two damaged bullets and held them up for Hodgins to see. "One from Mr. Buckingham, the other from Murphy. Grab that magnifying glass, will you?"

Stonehouse turned the two bullets and told Hodgins to look at them through the magnifier. "See that nick? It's on both bullets and they're identical. Caused by some sort of damage to the barrel of the gun. No doubt in my mind both were fired from the same weapon."

"That's a great help. Now, all I need to do is find the gun. Half the city has a weapon, and all the farmers have them. Problem will be finding the right one. Thank you." Hodgins folded the sheet containing the new information, stuffed it in his pocket, and headed back to the station.

* * *

Barnes called the detective over. "Sir, I found something."

Hodgins joined Barnes at the constable's desk. "What do you have, Henry?"

"I checked with the stockyard. I remember Charlie had a fair number of cattle and thought he may have purchased them there. He added another dozen to his herd and hasn't paid for them yet."

He looked at his notes. "Over seven hundred for the cattle and almost a hundred for a bull. I went to some of the farm implement companies. Owes a few hundred there. And he also had bills at the lumber mill and granary. Settled those bills a few weeks ago."

"Not surprised. He owed quite a bit of money to Kavanagh. Probably got the loan to pay some of his debts. So both Charlie and McTaggart are at the top of the list. Both owed money to Kavanagh's and Murphy's business in one form or another. McTaggart benefits from Murphy's death as the debit died with him, but Charlie isn't as lucky. His was a loan with Kavanagh. Both had motive to murder Mr. Buckingham, but Charlie benefitted the most. The bullets that killed both men are from a common gun, but Doctor Stonehouse noticed something to tie the two murders together."

"I know it's a bit of a stretch, sir, but what about Mr. Logan? He has managed to purchase the property he took Bucky to court about. He's not all that old and seems quite strong."

Hodgins raised an eyebrow. "That's an awful lot to go through for ten acres of land." He held a hand up as Barnes began to protest. "But I agree. He can't be ruled out. May as well check his finances. Who knows? Maybe he owed money to Murphy and Kavanagh as well."

Hodgins pulled out his pocket watch.

"It's getting late. First thing in the morning, I want you to bring in Charlie for questioning. Riddell needs to bring in McTaggart. And go separately. Don't want any more bother between Riddell and Buckingham."

CHAPTER NINETEEN

Cordelia knelt by the fence tending to her flower garden when her neighbour called over to her. She stood and removed her gloves. "Good afternoon, Margaret. You must be excited with the up-coming weddings."

"I've never been in such a state. Planning Bridget's wedding is one thing, but now everything has to be doubled. So many more people attending. The church will be overflowing, and I don't know what I'm going to do about the party afterwards."

Margaret paced along the fence waving her arms. "We were planning on having an intimate gathering here in our back garden. Most of Bridget's friends have married and long since moved away. Now with our Violet getting wed, all her friends will be in attendance. As will Henry's, along with several of his fellow constables. I just don't know what to do."

Violet and her aunt had agreed to have a double wedding. It was something that rarely happened in the city and the news spread quickly. Since Aunt Bridget's wedding date had already been set and passage for their departure to Europe booked two days later, instead of a traditional June wedding, both couples would be wed on May 22. Only one week left to expand on the event. Most of the planning had already been taken care of, they just needed to make a few changes to the gathering after the church service.

Cordelia set down her trowel. "Come through the gate. We'll have a cup of tea and figure this out." She waited while her neighbour, and now close friend, crossed through the opening in the fence. "Let's sit in the kitchen and decide what to do." Once the kettle had boiled and the tea made, Cordelia found a piece of paper and pencil and prepared to make notes.

"Now, what have you already planned? Once I know that we can figure out how to expand to accommodate the young folk."

Margaret took a long drink of tea, then leaned back. "Let see. Bridget won't be wearing a traditional wedding gown. Not at her age. I realize that older woman should be wed in black, but that just seems so drab. We've compromised and she'll be wearing a lovey gown in cinnamon. That colour compliments her skin tone. We've almost finished cutting the fabric, but it needs to be fitted and sewn, and now I have to make Violet's gown. I just don't know when I'll find the time."

Cordelia wrote the first item on her paper. "Not to worry. If you and Bridget have no objections, I can finish her gown while you start on Violet's. Do you have the fabric for your daughter's gown?"

Margaret shook her head. "I've been in such a tizzy I haven't had time."

"Not to worry. If you and Violet have no appointments, we can go this afternoon and pick out some lovely fabric. What does Violet prefer? Silk, organdy, linen, lace, gauze, tulle? Maybe cashmere? No, that would be too warm. What did you wear?"

Margaret giggled. "George and I eloped. Mother didn't approve, but she's come around."

Cordelia laughed. "My mother felt the same about Bertie, but didn't interfere. She's accepted him even though she won't admit it. She just can't get over the fact he didn't finish law school. It's a shame you don't have a gown to pass down. I just hope when Sara's time comes, she'll want to wear mine. So, that's taken care of. What else has you in a tizzy?"

"Where do I start? Wedding cake. Food. Invitations. Where to hold all those people. It will have to be a much larger place, so there will be even more decorations required."

Cordelia thought for a moment. "You said you were planning a small gathering in your back garden for Bridget?"

Margaret nodded.

"Why not have it in both our back gardens? We can have a portion of the fence taken down so people can wander back and forth. I'm certain Bertie won't mind."

"Oh, Cordelia. Would you? That would be such a help. And your garden is so nice. I was going to ask if you'd mind if Bridget could have a photograph taken under your apple tree. The blooms are lovely."

"Certainly. I just hope they stay long enough. What's next on the list." Cordelia looked at her paper. "The wedding cake. What did you have in mind?"

"For Bridget, a simple one-layer cake, with white icing and pink roses, to match her bouquet. That will never do for Violet. She's always dreamed of a tall cake, adorned with violets, of course. I don't know how I'll manage both."

"Not to worry. If you agree, I can do some of the baking, and Sara will want to help. We can do it all if you wish, and bring them over for you to decorate."

Margaret's eyes glistened as tears formed. "I'm so lucky you moved in next door. I don't know what I'd do without your friendship."

"Oh, pish-posh. You're more than capable of pulling this off. And I do enjoy having you as a friend. Now, dry your eyes and go home. See if Violet and Bridget are up for a shopping trip. We can spend the entire afternoon looking around Robert Simpson's store at Yonge and Queen Streets."

"Why don't you join us for luncheon? We can go shopping right after."

"I'll have to see if Mother can look after the twins. I'm certain she won't be busy. I'll take them over right away then join you."

* * *

"Thank you so much for helping, Mrs. Hodgins. I do so want Mama to make my gown and I didn't know how she'd find the time. I've never sewn anything so fancy, and I'd make such a mess of it on my own. Aunt Bridget's dress is almost ready." Violet talked so much she hardly ate anything on her plate.

Bridget turned to Cordelia. "I appreciate all your help. I can do a lot of the work on my dress, but an extra pair of hands would make it so much quicker. I'm looking forward to shopping for Violet's fabric. Did Margaret tell you about the lace?"

Cordelia looked puzzled. "Lace? You've already begun shopping then?"

Margaret shook her head. "No. It's some lace that George's mother had. We thought it would be perfect to trim Violet's dress with. I'll bring it along with us."

Mrs. Halloway hired a carriage to take them down town. When they arrived, she asked the driver to come back for them in an hour. He helped them down, and agreed to return after seeing the large tip she placed in his hand.

Violet stood on the walkway staring at the door. "I can't believe I'll be Mrs. Henry Barnes in a few weeks.

It's both exciting, and terrifying."

Mrs. Halloway put her arm around Violet's shoulders. "It is exciting, and there's nothing to be afraid of. You and Henry are perfect for each other. Now let's get that fabric so we can start on your dress. You'll be the most beautiful bride." She turned to her sister-in-law. "You'll both be beautiful."

They entered the store and went straight to the fabric department.

"Oh my. So much to choose from." Violet ran her fingers over several bolts of fabric as she slowly walked down the aisle.

A salesman came over. "How may I assist you ladies today?"

"My daughter is getting married and we need fabric for her gown."

The salesman smiled. "Congratulations. This way. We have the largest selections of silks, linen, and of course lace."

Cordelia followed, imaging a similar future trip with Sara.

Violet examined each carefully. "The silk is so soft, but I believe I want organdy."

"Excellent choice." He pulled a large bolt of white organdy from the shelf and walked to the next aisle. "This lace would complement it nicely."

Cordelia looked at the lace, then whispered to Margaret.

Margaret nodded and pulled the lace from her reticule. "I have this piece. It was her grandmother's. I don't believe it's near enough, though."

The salesman examined it. "I have just the thing. This way." He led them to the end of the aisle and showed them some lace that matched exactly.

"Don't forget she'll need a veil," Cordelia said.

"Oh, yes." Margaret turned to the salesman. "Where can we find the gauze?"

Once everything for Violet's gown had been paid for they looked around the rest of the store.

"I'll have to purchase a dress for the wedding. There's simply no time to make one. They have some beautiful ones here. I'll come back another day and choose one."

"Why not get one now, Mamma?"

"It's getting late, and I have a surprise at home I want to show you. Tonight we'll have to write out your invitations so we can take them to the printer."

* * *

When Hodgins got home, the house was filled with the aroma of his favourite meal; roast beef, carrots, potatoes, and biscuits with peach preserves. "What's the occasion? Or should I ask, what is it you want?" He kissed Cordelia and stole a piece of carrot.

"Whatever do you mean? Can I not cook a special meal just because I want to?" She laughed when he cocked his head and grinned. "There is something I wanted to tell you, but it won't cost a thing. I promise."

"Let me sit down before you spring it on me." He pulled one of the chairs away from the table and turned it towards the counter. "Ready. What do you want?"

"Why, I don't want anything. Except to help. Margaret is in such a dither trying to prepare for a double wedding. She mentioned they wouldn't be able to fit everyone into their garden for the after-party, so I said she could use ours, too."

Hodgins nodded. "And are the guests all supposed to squeeze through the gate or simply climb over the fence?"

Cordelia threw a towel at him then placed her

hands on her hips. "No one will be climbing over the fence. I told her you'd remove some of the boards to join the lawns."

"Not to worry. Henry's already been talking about the guest list. Between Violet's friends and all the coppers he plans on inviting, we might need to take down the fence on the other side as well."

"Why, I hadn't thought of that. The Cooper's will be leaving for Michigan in a few days. Her mother isn't well. They'll be gone for months. I'll mention it to Margaret and she can ask if that would be all right."

"Whoa. I was just kidding."

"I know, but as you said, Henry will be inviting a lot of his friends and fellow officers. Violet has a lot of friends, and they'll all be accompanied by their beaus or spouses. We can't have all those people crammed into two yards."

Hodgins threw up his hands in defeat. "I'm sorry I spoke. I should have known better. What else have you promised Margaret? Our entire house perhaps?"

"Well, I offered to help with the wedding gown. Only Bridget's. With both of us working on it, it'll be finished in no time, then she can help Margaret finish up Violet's. Oh, and I'll be baking cakes for the wedding, with a little help from Sara. Margaret will do the decorating. She's quite good at that, but she won't have time to both bake and then decorate the two cakes."

Hodgins stood and walked over to Cordelia. "I'll do my part and take Scraps out while you're baking. Don't want any accidents. And I'll volunteer Henry to help take down the fence. It is his wedding after all. It's the least he can do. I can't believe I'm saying this, but maybe your mother could come over to help as well."

Cordelia hugged him. "I just knew you'd agree. I'll ask Mother. Both houses will have to be cleaned from top to bottom, in the event of rain. And she can watch over the twins while I'm sewing and baking."

"Speaking of the twins, have you had any time to find a nanny?"

"Violet mentioned one of her friends. She's coming over tomorrow. I'll see how she gets along with the children. If I find her agreeable, I'll ask her to start right away."

"I'm glad something is working out. Now, if I can get so lucky with these murders. I can't decide if one person committed both, or if we're looking for two people. I'm certain they're connected. It's just too much of a coincidence that my main suspects know both of the deceased."

CHAPTER TWENTY

Hodgins arrived at the station house at the same time as Barnes. "Did you find anything on Logan?"

"Yes, sir. You were right thinking him not guilty of the murder. He owes nothing that I could find."

"And you were right to remind me not to dismiss anyone without investigating them thoroughly. So, we're back to Buckingham and McTaggart."

Hodgins looked around the station. "Riddell not about yet?"

"Told him to pick up supplies on his way in. Getting low on tea and biscuits. Should be here any time."

"When he arrives, I'll need him to fetch McTaggart. You go and get Buckingham. I want to speak with both. I'm certain one of them must have done it. Possibly even both, but without a confession or the weapon we have nothing. You go get Buckingham, sharpish."

Fifteen minutes after Barnes left, Riddell showed up. Hodgins followed him into the supply room.

"Put that stuff away and bring in McTaggart. I need to question him again."

"Yes, sir. Right away." Riddell put the tea and biscuits on the counter and hurried out the station door.

Hodgins sat at his desk reviewing his notes, shaking his head, and mumbling.

An hour later Barnes came in with an irate Charlie Buckingham. Hodgins let him sit alone in the interrogation room for almost thirty minutes before joining him. Charlie was more than a little perturbed. He drummed his fingers on the table, and his eyes narrowed as he spoke to Hodgins.

"What is it now? You've arrested me once and had to release me."

"You've not been arrested this time. I just need to clear up a few things." Hodgins riffled through his notes, prolonging the interview. "I see you've piled up quite a few debts."

Charlie banged his fists on the table top. "My finances are of no concern to the Toronto Constabulary. How dare you look into my personal business!"

"I'm investigating a murder. I have every right. Especially when your personal business makes you a very interesting suspect. You've inherited a large piece of property. Selling off pieces of it will help pay your bills. You'll have to sell more than the little chunk Logan bought in order to pay off the loan from Kavanagh. It's gotten quite high, and the longer you let it go, the more you'll owe. Won't take long before it's completely unmanageable."

Charlie stood, knocking the chair over. "If you're not arresting me, this interview is over. I'll see you lose your badge if you continue to harass me."

Hodgins spread his hands. "You're free to go any time. I'd have thought you'd want me to find out who murdered your father, but if you won't answer my questions, well, I can't control what people might have to say about that." He leaned back, balancing on the back legs of the chair.

"Are you threatening me, Detective?"

"Not at all. As I said, you're free to go any time, but I will be sending someone out to search your property."

Charlie left the interrogation room, the door slamming against the wall. Hodgins followed him to the front of the station house. Riddell was waiting, alone.

"Riddell, where's McTaggart?"

"Gone, sir. Took the early train to Kleinberg. His wife said he had to finish setting up the chemists shop."

"Damn! I know there's a later train, but I'll have to stay over. I suppose I could hire a carriage, but I'd still end up overnight. Don't relish travelling on those roads in the dark. Probably end up half way to Sarnia. I'll have to wait 'til morning and hope he hasn't scarpered. Why didn't I have someone keep an eye on the trains for more than one day? Especially since he mentioned taking the train the day after the funeral."

Hodgins turned. "Barnes, I want you to search Charlie's property immediately. Find that damn gun!" He banged his fist on the nearest desk. "Damn sloppy job. First Riddell gets into a brawl with one suspect, then the other one slips out of town un-noticed. Can't have it. There's going to be some changes around here. We're supposed to be protecting the citizens of Toronto. If the Inspector won't do something, by God I'll make damn sure the men under me toe the line."

Hodgins stomped into his office, slamming the door behind him, causing everyone to jump. One constable dropped his tea, sending slivers of china everywhere.

Everyone in the room stared in shock at the sudden outburst.

A minute later Hodgins opened his door and hollered. "Richardson, Barnes, go search the farm again. Look under every piece of straw if you have to."

The constables nodded and ran out the door, the remaining officers stood around mumbling.

* * *

The sun hung low by the time Barnes and Richardson arrived at Charlie Buckingham's farm. They spotted Charlie in one of the fields, facing away from the farmhouse.

"Let's see if the wife is in. She may be more cooperative than her husband." Barnes tied the horses to a post and motioned for Richardson to follow him.

Adelia answered the door right away. "Charlie is in the field." She stepped out and made to call him.

"No, please don't call him in yet. We'd like to speak with you alone for a moment, if you don't mind." Barnes bit his lower lip, hoping she wouldn't call to her husband.

She glanced towards Charlie, still preoccupied with a section of fence. "Please, come in. Can I offer you something? Tea and cake?"

"Temping as it is, we'll have to decline. We're here on business. I'm afraid we need to search your house and property."

"Search? Whatever for?"

Richardson stepped forward. "A gun, ma'am."

Adelia laughed. The sound was soft and reminded Barnes of a little mouse.

"Ma'am? Why is that funny?" Barnes and Richardson exchanged confused looks.

"Forgive me. It's just that my husband has a small collection of guns. You'll have to be more specific. Are you looking for a long gun, or a pistol?"

Barnes raised an eyebrow. "Does he now?

Wouldn't happen to have a .22 in the collection?"

"Why yes. A Smith and Wesson short black powder. A pair of them actually. Not the best topic of discussion for a woman, but Charlie does go on about them. I suppose I've learned more than I care to know."

"May we see them?" Richardson asked.

"I'll fetch them for you. Won't be a moment."

Floor boards creaked above as Adelia moved about. She returned with two hand guns. "Here they are."

Barnes indicated for Richardson to take them. "We'll need to keep these for a bit." He opened his notebook, tore out a fresh page, and wrote on it. "Here's a receipt for them." Barnes handed the paper to Adelia then turned to Richardson. "We may have just got lucky and saved a lot of bother."

He thanked Adelia for her time and cooperation and raced the horses back to the livery. They ran to the station house only to be told Hodgins had just left for home.

"I'll see if I can catch him." Barnes ran out, hoping Hodgins walked his usual route. He found him only a few blocks away.

"Sir." Barnes paused to catch his breath. "We got two Smith and Wesson's from Charlie's wife."

"Good lad." Hodgins turned and walked with a huffing Barnes back to Station Four. "You really do need to start training."

"Yes, sir. Right after the honeymoon."

"Might want to get fit before the wedding." Hodgins laughed and slapped Barnes on the back.

When they walked into the station, Richardson brought over the two hand guns. Hodgins took one and examined it.

"We need to check the bullets. Need something to fire them into. Something not too hard. Bale of straw perhaps? Richardson, go to the livery and fetch one.

Twenty minutes later Hodgins, Barnes, Richardson, and a few curious constables stood in the alley beside Station House Four, a bale of straw snuggled up against the wall. Barnes put one bullet in each gun and handed the first to Hodgins. He fired it into the bale, then took the second and did the same. Two constables searched through the straw while Hodgins held up a pair of lanterns. It took over thirty minutes to find both bullets.

Hodgins took them into his office and examined them under a magnifying glass, looking for a nick.

"Got it!"

All heads turned.

"Barnes, I need you to arrest Charlie, hopefully for the last time. Go to the livery and hitch up the police wagon.

* * *

Hodgins pushed the team of horses almost to the point of collapse. Dust kicked up as they raced along the lane to Charlie Buckingham's farm. One wheel of the paddy wagon hit a rut. If he hadn't been holding tight, Barnes would've landed on the ground when the wagon tipped. Hodgins pulled on the reins. Both horses reared at the sudden stop.

A scream pierced the air.

Barnes leapt off before the wagon came to a halt. In his haste, he tripped on the porch steps, allowing Hodgins to catch up. Hodgins threw open the door. Adelia lay crumpled on the kitchen floor among pieces of a broken chair.

Hodgins lunged at Charlie. Barnes rushed to the

woman's aid. "What have you done?"

The two men rolled when Hodgins made contact. "Barnes, is she—"

"Alive, sir, but badly injured."

Hodgins straddled Charlie, knee digging into his back. "Why?"

"Stupid bitch gave you my guns."

Hodgins dug his knee deeper. "Charlie Buckingham, I'm arresting you for the murder of your father and Mr. Murphy, and the attempted murder of your wife."

Barnes tossed Hodgins his handcuffs. The detective dragged Charlie to the police wagon, locking him in the back.

"You can't do this. I needed the farm so I could clear my debts. Why can't you see it was the only way? My father wouldn't have lasted much longer. I simply put him out of his misery. I'd do the same for any dying animal." He grabbed the bars, shaking them so hard they rattled.

"I'm not taking the blame for killing that leech of a pawn broker. I spent the entire day with my bank, trying to find a way to save my farm. Ask him."

"You could have shot him after you left the bank. Coroner can't say exactly when he died. I'll talk to your banker tomorrow as a formality, but Murphy was killed with your gun. That I can prove." Hodgins turned and went back inside, smiling as Charlie continued to yell insults.

"She's coming around." Barns sat on the floor beside her. A towel elevated her head.

"I've no doubt you'll be an outstanding husband. She needs medical attention. Hitch up one of their horses and buggy and take her over to her mother-in-law's. Drive slow. I'll send back a doctor. I believe Mrs. Buckingham has been released from the hospital. Hopefully, Adelia doesn't need to be admitted. Beatrice will have her hands full tending to two women assaulted by Charlie."

* * *

After locking Charlie into a cell, Hodgins sat in his office waiting for Barnes to return with news of Adelia. When Barnes had tried to clean the wound on her temple, Hodgins had noticed bits of wood from the chair in her hair and over the clothing. He assumed the doctor would need to stitch her up.

Over an hour later, Barnes finally came through the front door.

"She's resting comfortably. Mrs. McTaggart is going to stay as long as necessary, nursing her mother and Adelia back to health. She's even going to see if she can convince Adelia to sell the farm to pay off the debts and move to Kleinburg with her. Are you still planning on going there in the morning to see Mr. McTaggart?"

Hodgins shook his head. "No. Charlie has confessed he killed his father to get his hands on the property, but he swears he didn't kill Murphy. McTaggart wouldn't have been able to get the gun, kill Murphy, then return it. Now off home with you. It's been a long day."

Hodgins left shortly after Barnes, taking his time. He had a peculiar feeling Charlie told the truth about not killing Murphy. He confessed to one murder, so why not both?

When he arrived home, he went straight to the front room and paced by the fireplace. A fire burned as the evening chill had set in for the night. He stopped when Cordelia spoke.

"Bertie, is something wrong? Not so much as a hello from you."

He crossed the room and kissed her. "Sorry, Delia. Thought I had these two murders solved. Charlie admitted killing his father for the farm, but not the pawn broker. Why? It's not as though we can hang him twice."

Cordelia took his arm and guided him to one of the chair's by the fire. She sat in the other. "Are you absolutely certain he killed both?"

Hodgins leaned back staring at the ceiling. "I thought so. Both bullets came from the same gun. Dr. Stonehouse is positive the markings left by the gun barrel are unique."

Cordelia tapped her foot on the carpet, thinking. "No one else could have used the gun?"

Hodgins shook his head. "No. Charlie or Adelia were at the farm almost all of the time. The only time they both seemed to be out, they were at his mother's. All the suspects were present and could vouch for each other. I doubt a total stranger snuck in, stole the gun, shot Murphy, and put it back."

"So, if it wasn't Charlie ..." She waited while he

gave that some thought.

Hodgins bolted upright. "You're not suggesting what I think you are? But why?"

Cordelia smiled. "It was just a thought. Why don't you walk Scraps while I finish supper?"

Hodgins grabbed the leash, followed her into the kitchen, then joined the dog in the backyard.

"Come on, boy. Help me figure this one out." He led Scraps out the side gate and around the block. By the time they returned, he'd made a decision.

* * *

First thing in the morning Hodgins hired a shay from the livery and rode to the senior Buckingham's farm. He hesitated before knocking.

"Good morning, Detective. Please, come in."

"Thank you, Mrs. McTaggart. I'm sorry to intrude so early, but I need a word with Charlie's wife. Is she sufficiently recovered?"

"She's a little bruised and sore, but nothing's broken. She's in the kitchen with Mama."

I'd like to speak with her in private."

"Of course. I'll bring her to the parlour. You know the way."

Hodgins stood by the window while he waited, trying to decide how to approach her.

"Detective?"

He turned and gasped at the sight of Adelia's puffy, and blackened eyes. "Are … are you all right? I'm afraid I have several questions that can't wait."

"I've been expecting you." Adelia settled in the chair by the window, hands clasped in her lap. "You've figure it out, haven't you? I'll not make a fuss."

Hodgins sat on the chair opposite her. "Tell me what happened."

"You know that Charlie has a large loan with that horrid man at the pawn shop. I simply went down to ask if he couldn't wait a little longer for payment." Adelia dabbed her eyes with a lace hanky, wincing at the pain. "He wasn't there, but his partner was." She closed her eyes and shuttered.

Hodgins waited while she composed herself. His notebook rested on his knee, but he left it closed.

Adelia shook her head and opened her eyes. "I had Charlie's gun with me. The area isn't safe for a woman unaccompanied. That man took in my figure and came around the counter. Said if I was nice to him, he'd speak with Kavanagh. Then he grabbed me and started pawing at me. We were alone in the shop. I couldn't break free. The gun went off. I don't even recall pulling the trigger."

Hodgins leaned back, mulling over her confession. "Murphy attacked and you defended yourself. Your husband will hang for the murder of his father even if he continues to say he didn't kill Murphy. I see no reason to take this any further." He rose and put his notebook back into his pocket.

"Your sister-in-law has invited you to stay with them when they return to Kleinburg. I'd suggest you accept. Good day, Mrs. Buckingham."

CHAPTER TWENTY-ONE

Hodgins and his family joined Henry's mother and sister in the front pew, waiting for the wedding to begin. Mrs. Barnes sniffled and dabbed her eyes with a lacy hanky.

"I can't believe my little Henry is getting wed. And to such a beautiful young woman."

"Look at all the people, Mommy." Henry's sister twisted in her seat to see everyone in attendance.

The front pews were filled with family and close friends, but half the guests were strangers, curious to see a double wedding. It had become the event of the season and no one wanted to miss it.

Church and Davenport Streets were lined with well-wishers, waiting for the couples to exit after the service. A reporter for *The Globe* sat in the back pew, making copious notes on everyone's attire and the festive mood.

Both grooms stood at the front of the Primitive Methodist Church, almost identical in their attire. They wore white frock coats, with a flower in the lapel. A violet for Henry and a pink rose for Frederick to match their bride's bouquets. They looked quite dapper with their lavender, doe-skinned trousers. The organist began to play and all heads turned to watch the brides come down the aisle.

George Halloway acted as both father of the bride and stand-in father for his sister. His outfit was similar to the groom's, except he wore a cornflower blue frock coat and grey trousers, with a white rose in the lapel. He walked down the aisle with his daughter on his left and his sister on his right. His smile couldn't have been any wider.

The ceremony lasted a little over an hour, then everyone scurried out the door to shower the two new couples with white rice and grains, endowing a wish of fertility on the newlyweds. Two carriages waited, each pulled by a team of white horses, ready to whisk the couples back to the Halloway's for a celebratory brunch.

* * *

Hodgins' mother-in-law made a last-minute check, making certain all three back gardens were perfect. Euphemia didn't know Henry or the Halloway's very well, so she wasn't upset at missing the wedding. Besides, both she and her husband, Harold, preferred to play with the twins.

Harold took on the role of nanny while Euphemia went next door to fuss over the food and decorations. When she heard the buggies coming down the street, she scurried out the back door and joined her husband at the Hodgins' residence.

The photographer set up in front of the apple tree, which was heavily laden with scented blossoms. It seemed twice as full as the day before, as though the tree waited for the wedding to display its full glory.

* * *

Hodgins found a few minutes to speak with Henry while the guests fussed over the two brides.

"Any last-minute advice, sir?"

Hodgins placed a hand on Henry's shoulder. "Always treat her with respect, listen to what she has to say, and never take her for granted." He paused a moment before continuing. "Most important, scrimp and save, and get out of her parent's house as soon as possible."

Henry smiled. "No disrespect, but my mother-in-law isn't like yours. Besides, Mr. Halloway just told us he's giving us a house as a wedding present. A small cottage, but it's all ours."

"Wonderful news. Now, get back to your new bride."

ABOUT THE AUTHOR

Nanci M. Pattenden is a genealogist and an emerging fiction writer, currently working on a collection of detective stories set in Victorian Toronto. She also co-authors a funny paranormal series, D.E.M.ON. Tales.

She has completed the Creative Writing program at both the University of Calgary and the University of Toronto.

Nanci currently resides in Newmarket with her fluffy cat Snowball.

nanci@nancipattenden.com
www.murderdoespayink.ca
www.nancipattenden.com
@npattenden